A CHEERFUL LITTLE COLORING DAY

Holidays at Rawhide Ranch

PAIGE MICHAELS

By Paige Michaels

©All rights reserved.

This is a work of fiction. Names, characters, businesses, places, events, and incidents are either the products of the author's imagination or used in a fictitious manner. Any resemblance to actual persons, living or dead, or actual events is purely coincidental.

No part of the book may be reproduced or transmitted in any form or by any means, electronic or mechanical, including photocopying, recording, or by any information storage and retrieval system, without permission in writing from the publisher.

2022 © Published by Paige Michaels

Holidays at Rawhide Ranch

A Cheerful Little Coloring Day

Edited by Maggie Ryan

Cover by AllyCat's Creations

This book is intended for adults only. Spanking and other sexual activities represented in this book are fantasies only, intended for adults. Nothing in this book should be interpreted as the author's advocating any non-consensual spanking/sexual activity or the spanking of minors.

For more Rawhide Ranch stories check out this link-
https://linktr.ee/Rawhide

❦ Created with Vellum

ACKNOWLEDGMENTS

A huge thank you to Allie Belle for inviting me to write in her Rawhide Ranch series yet again! It was so much fun playing in her world and joining all the other authors who have come before me!

CHAPTER ONE

"Eloise Grace, what on Earth are you doing out here in the middle of the night?"

The stern, authoritative voice caused Eloise to jerk her gaze from where she was toeing the sand in the sandbox to face the night security guard at Rawhide Ranch. "I couldn't sleep," she said, hearing the defiance in her voice. Lately, she felt like everything she said had a tone of rebelliousness.

Master Rhodes Taft frowned down at her, hands on his hips. He oozed authoritative dominance that made her tremble. "You know good and well that Little girls are not permitted to leave the Littles' wing after light's out."

She shrugged. "I wanted to feel the cool sand on my toes. It gets hot during the day. At night it feels like the beach. Or at least how I imagine the beach would feel." She mumbled that last part. She'd never been to the beach or seen the ocean.

Master Rhodes squatted down next to her, but he was so large and imposing it didn't put him at her level at all. "If

Master Derek finds out you were out here breaking all the rules, he will tan your hide good, little one."

Eloise shrugged. "Don't care." She did care though. If she were honest with herself, she'd not only hoped she would get caught out roaming around tonight, but she'd also hoped it would be Master Rhodes who found her.

Either Master Rhodes or Master Tiago Murray. Both of them were smolderingly hot Daddy types who made her heart race. Both of them worked for security. The chances of one of them being on the night shift and catching her outside were pretty high.

Now what? She had a reputation as a very naughty girl at Rawhide Ranch. Now that it was established, she had very little trouble maintaining it. The cost was high though. She was lonely and sad. She also made everyone around her frustrated.

"Is that so?" Master Rhodes turned slightly so he was sitting next to her on the edge of the sandbox. "Why's that, little one? Is something bothering you?" His thigh brushed against hers for a fleeting second, making her breath hitch.

"Doesn't matter," she grumbled. Why would Master Rhodes or anyone else care if something was bothering her? She'd been living here on the Ranch for a while now and she still wasn't sure why Master Derek let her stay.

Sure, she found Master Rhodes to be unbelievably attractive, but that wouldn't be reciprocated in a million years. To him, she would be nothing more than an annoying Little girl.

To *her*, Master Rhodes was larger than life. A fantasy. Someone she thought about late at night when she was alone in her bed in the dark. He was strict and firm, but he was also kind. He smiled at her every time she saw him. He made her feel special.

She wasn't, of course. She was just one of many Little

A CHEERFUL LITTLE COLORING DAY

girls who lived at the ranch because Master Derek took her in and gave her a place to live. But kindness wasn't something she'd experienced many times in her twenty-four years, so it mattered to her.

He wasn't the only one. Master Tiago was her other fantasy Daddy. Whereas Master Rhodes had dark hair, brown eyes, and tanned skin, Master Tiago had dirty-blond hair and blue eyes. He wasn't quite as tall as Master Rhodes, or as broad, but they were both over six foot and dwarfed her.

Master Rhodes nudged her with his knee. "It matters to me, Eloise. How about you tell me? Maybe I can help."

Eloise glanced at him. He didn't mean it. He was just being kind. Again. Why would he want to help out a naughty Little girl like her who couldn't go one day without breaking the rules? She hmphed.

"Have you ever had your own Daddy, little one?" he asked in a gentle voice.

She shook her head. "Nobody wants me."

Master Rhodes flinched next to her. "Now, I don't believe that. You just haven't found the right Daddy yet is all."

Sometimes Eloise felt like the actual orphan she'd been most of her life. Like no one would ever adopt her. They hadn't. And no Daddy was ever going to want her either. She wasn't the sort of girl who got chosen.

She watched out of her peripheral vision as Master Rhodes bent over to remove his shoes and socks. A moment later, he dug his toes into the cool sand next to her. "Huh... That does feel nice."

She glanced up at him. "Have you ever been to the beach?"

He nodded. "It's been a long time, but I have. You're

right. At night the sand feels cool on your tootsies just like this."

Eloise sighed. She'd never get to go to the beach. It wasn't in the cards for her. She didn't have that kind of luck. The most she could hope for in life would be to someday own her own television so she could flip through the channels and at least choose a show that took place at the beach.

"I hate that you're so sad, Eloise. I'd like to help if you'll let me."

"How?" She glanced at him again. He was so very handsome and, even sitting, he towered over her. Six-two with broad shoulders. Even if she got in a heap of trouble, it would be worth it.

"Maybe we could spend some time together. Perhaps if you got to know me better, we could become friends and then you'd have someone you could talk to about your feelings."

She shook her head almost before he finished speaking. No way did she want to spend time with this handsome Daddy. It would only make things worse when he eventually grew tired of her and walked away.

Then what are you doing out here in the middle of the night?

People always lied to her. They told her they would be her friend and then they changed their minds when they got to know her better. She wasn't likeable. She knew it. Her life was proof of that fact.

Master Rhodes sighed. "That makes me sad. Why don't you want to spend time with me? Am I not likeable or funny enough? Am I ugly?" He was teasing.

She gasped and jerked her gaze to his again. "Don't be absurd. You're the handsomest, kindest, funniest man at the Ranch." She slapped her palm over her mouth as soon as those words came out. What was she thinking?

Master Rhodes gave her a slow smile. "Now we're getting somewhere. So, I'm handsome, huh?"

She rolled her eyes and turned back to face the sand.

Master Rhodes reached over and stroked under her chin with two fingers. "Look at me, little one."

She sighed as she did so. "What?" she asked, making sure her voice was as sassy as possible. She'd obviously slipped from her usual surly personality for a moment. She needed to regain control. If she didn't, she would get hurt.

He searched her eyes. "I know you've had a rough life and it hasn't been easy assimilating to life at Rawhide Ranch, but you're the prettiest Little girl I've ever seen when you're not scowling. I bet if you gave someone a chance to be your friend, you could find a way to stop misbehaving and possibly even smile."

She rolled her eyes again. It was a habit. "You're just saying that to be nice because you have to. You work here. I know I'm not likeable or pretty. You don't have to humor me."

Master Rhodes's eyes went wide with shock. "That's not true at all, little one. I don't have to be nice to you if I don't want to. I could have dragged you back to the Littles' dorm, woken Master Derek up, and had him discipline you ten minutes ago if I'd wanted."

Eloise shivered. The idea wasn't unappealing. She never told anyone this, but she actually liked it when Master Derek spanked her. At least it meant someone noticed her and paid attention when she misbehaved. It was far better than always being the good girl. The wallflower.

Eloise hardly cared that no one liked her. She was used to that. Even her parents hadn't liked her. They'd left her on the doorstep of a church when she was three years old. At least they'd had the decency to leave her there during the day when someone was actually at the church. They'd also found enough kindness in them to ring the bell before tearing off and leaving her orphaned.

Her first and second foster families hadn't liked her either. She'd been a difficult child, always getting into trouble until no one could handle her, and then she went back into the system.

The system was broken. Eloise knew this more than anyone. When she was fifteen, she'd walked away from the group home where she'd been living and never looked back. More importantly, as far as she'd known, no one had ever searched for her.

Eloise was no one. Just a body with no family and no real friends. She was bitter and angry, and well aware of those facts.

Master Rhodes lifted her chin again. She'd gone so far into her head she'd almost forgotten where she was or who she was with. "I don't know the details about your past, little one, but I bet you've had a rough life. I know you grew up in foster care and group homes. That must have been hard and lonely and probably felt like no one rooted for you. I bet you could use someone on your team. Team Eloise Grace. I'd like to be that person. If you'll let me. And you know what?" He didn't wait for her to respond before he continued, "Master Tiago would like to be there for you too."

For a moment, Eloise blinked at the huge Daddy who was staring earnestly into her eyes. He looked so sincere. He probably even meant what he was saying. Both of them?

Eloise knew better than to trust anyone. People always said things and then took them back. Master Rhodes would too. He might have thought he could be her friend, but he would tire of her like everyone else. He would grow exasperated with her antics.

She couldn't face his kind eyes anymore. They made

promises he wouldn't keep. They teased her with hope that would poof out of the air in a heartbeat.

Unwilling to face him another moment, she jumped to her feet and took off running toward the dorm. She ran hard so he couldn't catch her, though she could sense he wasn't following.

She was panting by the time she reached the back door to the Littles' wing. Scampering up the stairs to the third floor, she walked down the hallway as quietly as she could and eased open the door to the room she shared with three other Littles.

A noise caused her to pause on the threshold and hold her breath as the girl in the nearest bed turned over to her other side. Once Nat was still, and Eloise was sure all three of her roomies were sound asleep, she tiptoed back into her room and climbed under the covers. Even if they hadn't been, she doubted they would have paid any attention to her. They barely spoke to her on a good day. They wouldn't care what she'd done to get into trouble in the middle of the night.

She couldn't blame them. She had tantrums in the nursery and threw the blocks or kicked over other people's towers. She was mean. She couldn't stop herself.

Eloise held back her tears as she grabbed Peaches, her stuffed bunny, and hugged her bestest friend close to her chest. Peaches was the only friend she had who never judged her or made her feel inadequate or unlovable. Peaches always smiled and comforted her.

Peaches was also the only possession Eloise had from her childhood. The stuffie had been in her hands when her parents abandoned her, and she'd gone through every foster home and group home and later homeless shelter alongside her.

The one and only time Eloise stepped over the line and

became actually destructive in her life had been a day when she'd been fourteen and come home from school to the room she'd shared with five other girls in the group home to find Peaches missing from her bed.

In the end, it turned out that Peaches had fallen off the back side of the bed and gotten lodged between the mattress and the wall, but while Eloise was looking for her, she'd torn the entire room to shreds, thinking one of the other girls had taken her to be mean.

Eloise squeezed her eyes tight, trying to shake that memory away.

I'm not a bad person, she reminded herself.

It was hard to be good though. What was the point? Being naughty meant people paid attention to her. Even negative attention was better than nothing.

CHAPTER TWO

Eloise was tired the next morning when she showed up for work. After rotating through several different jobs at Rawhide Ranch, she'd found her niche a few months ago and settled into helping Chef Connor in the cafeteria.

With no experience doing much of anything, it had been hard for Eloise to know if she would like gardening or cleaning or hostessing or cooking. In the end, she'd found herself excited and eager to work in the kitchen. She especially loved creating cute desserts like parfaits or fruit tarts. She had an artistic side when it came to food.

The only time Eloise felt good about herself was when she overheard people talking about how pretty the desserts were. It was her only source of pride.

This morning she was in charge of pancakes. Those could be just as fun. She had perfected the batter amount until she was able to create perfect round circles that were always the same size. She stacked them in threes on the plates for the buffet line.

"Eloise?"

Eloise jerked her gaze toward Chef Connor to find him

frowning at her. When he pointed at the griddle in front of her, she glanced down to realize she'd poured enough batter onto it to fill the entire pan. "Shit," she muttered as she set the batter down and stared at her mistake.

"Little girl," he growled. "Language."

"Sorry, Sir," she said as she tried to figure out how to fix this mess. "I got distracted."

"Maybe that's because you didn't get enough sleep last night, ya think?" He was frowning at her.

Eloise swallowed hard. How did Chef Connor know about her antics last night?

"I came to tell you that Master Derek wants to see you in his office. I'll finish up the pancakes." He took the spatula from her and pointed toward the door. "Nanny J will escort you."

Eloise's shoulders dropped and she groaned. "Double shit."

"Language, little girl, language," he boomed.

Eloise dragged her feet on the way to the kitchen door. The last thing she wanted to do this morning was get reprimanded for sneaking out last night. She was too tired to deal with the repercussions.

No, that wasn't true. She'd known there was a good chance she would get caught and end up in Master Derek's office today, but she was feeling particularly feisty now because she suspected Master Rhodes had snitched on her, and that made her mad. It would just prove what she already knew to be true—Master Rhodes wasn't really her friend either.

A frowning Nanny J was waiting for Eloise when she stepped into the hallway. "You sure do enjoy getting spanked, little one," she said as she set her hand on Eloise's shoulder and turned her to face down the long hallway.

Eloise didn't say a word as she let Nanny J lead her out

A CHEERFUL LITTLE COLORING DAY

of the Littles' wing and across the lobby to Master Derek's office. She was still trying to come up with excuses for her latest antics as she stepped into the firm Ranch owner's office, jumping in place as Nanny J shut the door with a resounding snick.

Master Derek wasn't alone in the office. Master Rhodes was there. So was the other security guard she liked who worked on the Ranch, Master Tiago. *Shit*.

All three men were standing which made Eloise feel very small. She threaded her fingers together in front of her to keep from fidgeting.

Master Derek came around to the front of his desk, leaned his butt against it, and crossed his arms. He was frowning. Everyone was frowning today.

"Would you like to explain why you snuck out of the dorm last night to play at the playground?" Master Derek asked, his voice firm. He had a presence that brooked no argument but was never truly angry or scary. He wouldn't harm a flea, but he would discipline naughty Little girls, and he did so every day.

Eloise glanced at Master Rhodes and scowled. "Tattletale."

"Watch it, little one," Master Derek stated. "I don't think you're in a position to place blame. For the record, Master Rhodes didn't tell me he found you in the sandbox last night. I found out what you'd done from someone else."

Eloise jerked her gaze toward Master Derek. "Who?"

"That's not important. The point is that I called Master Rhodes in this morning to tell me what he knew because I was certain he would have a story. Nothing gets by him on night watch. Now, I'd like to hear it from you."

Eloise licked her lips. "I wanted to go to the beach," she murmured, well aware that sounded absurd.

"The beach?" Master Derek chuckled. "I've been trying to get you to enroll in classes to get your GED for months. I think you should give that more consideration if you think there's a beach in Montana."

Eloise narrowed her gaze and lifted her arms to cross them defiantly in front of her. "I know that."

Master Derek leaned his palms on the desk at either side of his hips and strummed his fingers along the edge. "Master Rhodes, Master Tiago, and I have been talking this morning."

Eloise gasped. "Are you going to kick me out?"

"Is that what you want?" Master Derek asked. "Is that why you misbehave all the time?"

Eloise chewed on her bottom lip, shaking her head. Her heart beat faster with fear. "Eventually you will anyway. Everyone does. Might as well get it over with."

Master Derek stared at her for several seconds before shaking his head. "We don't operate that way here, little one. No matter how defiant and naughty you are, as long as you aren't hurting anyone or yourself, you will not be asked to leave."

Eloise pursed her lips. Stupid tears gathered in the corners of her eyes, and she fought hard to keep them at bay. She lowered her gaze to the floor and held her breath.

Master Derek continued, "I'm fully aware that you're very unhappy, Eloise. Everyone knows as well. You make that clear to all the Littles and the Daddies every day. We all hate that for you. I run Rawhide Ranch with the intent of helping people. I want you to be healthy and happy and well-adjusted. I'm failing you, and that makes me sad."

Eloise jerked her gaze up to his and gasped. "It's not your fault I'm naughty," she pointed out. "I... I can't help myself."

"I know that, little one, but it makes me sad anyway."

He drew in a deep breath. "I think part of the problem is that you don't have a Daddy to help guide you and teach you how to make good decisions. Some Littles struggle when they're left to their own devices in the dorm. It can be especially hard for a Little like you who prefers a younger age than others."

Eloise had no idea where Master Derek was going with this chat, so she said nothing.

"I have a proposition for you."

She bit into her bottom lip again and blinked at him before glancing at the other two men. Somehow they played a role in this proposition.

"Would you like to sit, little one?" Master Derek asked.

She shook her head. She didn't want to get comfortable. She wanted to hear what he had to say.

"Okay then. Here it is. Master Rhodes and Master Tiago have offered to take you under their wings and help you find yourself. It would mean moving into their home at Rawhide Ridge and living under their rules instead of living in the dorm. I think this would be an excellent opportunity for you, Eloise."

Eloise gasped as she glanced around at all three men. No one moved.

Master Rhodes dipped his fingers into the front pockets of his pants and crossed his ankles.

"Why?" she asked softly. Her mind was running as she tried to picture this scenario. Move in with these two men? In their home? As what? Their Little? It was a horrible idea. She started shaking her head.

Master Rhodes took a deep breath. "Little one…"

Master Tiago cleared his throat. "Because we care about you, Eloise. We want you to find yourself and be happy and successful."

She kept shaking her head. "You can't."

"Can't what, little one?" Master Rhodes asked.

"Can't... care about me."

Master Tiago sucked in a breath. "Why on Earth not? I certainly care about you. I've been watching you for months. It breaks my heart that you're unhappy. I want to see you well-adjusted and excited about life."

Eloise stared at Master Tiago. He was just as handsome as Master Rhodes. He made her heart beat just as fast whenever she saw him.

"I can't move in with you," she reiterated, shifting her gaze back to Master Derek. "I can't, Sir. Please don't make me. I'll be good. I promise."

Master Derek ran a hand over his face. "I don't want you to be good, little one. I want you to be happy. If being naughty made you happy, I'd be the first to condone your behavior. The problem is neither being naughty nor being good makes you shine, Eloise. You're unhappy no matter what."

Her voice squeaked as she countered him. "I won't sneak out at night anymore. I promise. I won't throw my toys. I won't end up in your office every day. I can do it. I will."

Master Derek shifted his attention to Master Rhodes and Master Tiago. "Would you two mind giving me a few minutes alone with Eloise?"

"Of course," they both responded at once as they headed for the door and stepped out of the office, pulling the door closed behind them.

Eloise jumped.

"Sit, little one." Master Derek pointed at the chair in front of him before lowering himself into the one next to it. This time he wasn't making a suggestion. He meant for her to sit.

Eloise was shaking as she took her seat. She kept her

A CHEERFUL LITTLE COLORING DAY

hands threaded in her lap, staring at them. Emotions overwhelmed her. She was afraid Master Derek was going to make her say things she'd rather keep to herself.

"Talk to me, Eloise," he said gently. "Tell me why you don't want to accept help."

She jerked her gaze to his. "They... They're..." Her bottom lip was trembling, and she sucked in a breath and held it.

Master Derek leaned forward, setting his elbows on his knees so he was eye to eye with her. "Do you have a problem with either of them, Eloise?"

She shook her head, but then changed her mind and nodded.

"What's the problem, little one. Tell me."

She glanced at the door, praying Master Rhodes and Master Tiago wouldn't be able to hear her with it closed. She had waited outside that door many times while Master Derek was in here with someone. Even though she knew most of the time the Little in this office was getting his or her butt spanked, she'd never heard a single cry or whimper, but that didn't mean his office was totally soundproofed.

Master Derek sighed. "I've known Master Rhodes and Master Tiago for a long time, Little one. They're good friends and happen to share a house. They nearly always work different shifts which would make it easier for one of them to be with you at all times. You need structure and supervision and care. I think you need someone in your space as often as possible so that you're constantly reminded that you're worthy of being loved."

Eloise's breath hitched. She shook her head. "I'm not."

Master Derek's eyes shot wide. "Of course you are, Little one. Everyone deserves to be loved."

She shook her head again. "Not me." A tear escaped and

then another, making her angry that she was showing so much emotion.

Master Derek grabbed a tissue out of the box on the corner of his desk and handed it to her. "Including you, Eloise. Especially you. I know you've had a rough life. It wasn't fair. But you're a good person. Under that gruff exterior is a sweet Little girl who needs someone to love her."

She tried to suck in oxygen, but she was failing. More tears fell, and she swiped at them with the tissue. "I don't want anyone to love me, Sir," she whispered.

"Why not?"

Her entire body was trembling now. "Because it hurts worse when they leave."

Master Derek swallowed hard and reached for her hand, wrapping his much larger one around hers and holding it tight. "I hate that people have left you, Eloise. If I could go back in time and make sure you were loved as a child, I would stuff you in a time machine, find all those people, and beat them up for you." His voice was teasing, but also serious.

He continued, "No one should be unkind to a child. No one. It's cruel. But I'm offering you a second chance. Master Tiago and Master Rhodes are offering you a second chance. Don't turn it down. Let them show you that you're worthy and deserve to be happy."

She sniffled. "Can't you pick a Daddy who looks like a toad and smells bad and is mean?"

Master Derek chuckled, a deep rumbling that vibrated from his body up her arm. "Why would you want a mean, foul-smelling toad, Eloise?"

"Because I like Master Rhodes and Master Tiago. They're kind and funny and handsome. It will hurt more when they tire of me. I know because I've been down this

A CHEERFUL LITTLE COLORING DAY

road before. Eventually, they will not want to deal with me anymore, and then I'll feel worse than I do now."

Master Derek's expression was filled with compassion. "Master Rhodes and Master Tiago *are* very kind men. You're right. They're excellent Daddies too. They will not toss you out because you misbehave. I know because I had a very long talk with them before bringing this up to you."

"You can't know that." Her voice rose. "You can't know what people will do in the future."

He squeezed her hand. "I do know what people have done in your past, little one, and I'm asking you to take this chance. I'll make a deal with you."

She stared at him skeptically, not liking the direction this was going.

"You give them one month. A trial period. If at the end of one month, you don't think it's working, I'll move you back to the dorm and give you your own room and your job back."

Her eyes widened. "My job? You want me to stop working at the cafeteria?"

"I think you should take some time to concentrate on you without worrying about other responsibilities."

"But I like my job, Sir." Helping in the kitchen was the first time she'd ever really held an actual job, even if it wasn't fulltime and her room and board weren't dependent on working a certain number of hours or anything. It was the first job she'd been proud of and enjoyed.

"I'm so glad to hear that. I promise not to give it away. It will be there for you." He squeezed her hand again. "Eloise, look at me."

She met his gaze. She owed him that much. He'd saved her life more than once. He was letting her live here at Rawhide Ranch and doing everything he could to help her.

"I want you to trust me. I want you to take this chance, little one. Do it for yourself."

She swallowed hard and found herself nodding. It was hard to tell Master Derek no. He was the owner and a fair Master. She would do this. She wasn't sure how she would survive when Master Tiago and Master Rhodes grew tired of her, but she would try.

CHAPTER THREE

Eloise was quiet as she stepped into Master Tiago and Master Rhode's house. She was extremely nervous and unsure what to say to either of them. She was also overwhelmed. Suddenly, she had two Daddies in charge of her. She'd never even had one.

They weren't really *her* Daddies of course, but they were Daddies and she was meant to obey them.

The biggest problem was that she was attracted to these men. Both of them. How was she supposed to stay in their home and pretend they were her caregivers when she was infatuated with both of them? They would be horrified if they found out.

Eloise had spent enough time with the counselors at Rawhide Ranch to understand the reason why she was Little. She'd come to realize that people liked to live as a much younger girl for a variety of reasons, but for Eloise, it was simple. She'd never really had her own childhood.

Sure, she'd been young. She'd occasionally had a birthday party at one of the foster homes. She'd had some toys and books she could play with along the way. But what she'd really missed out on was a loving caregiver who gave a shit about her.

That was the appeal. So, she'd gone into her head years ago and begun to pretend that she was a Little girl with parents who adored her and doted on her. It had been her safe place. Her happy place. It was pretend, but it got her through life.

Now that she was twenty-four, a full-grown adult, she still liked to spend most of her time in a much younger headspace. It wasn't easy when no one truly took care of her and she had to pretend they did, but she'd eventually decided it was safer that way. It kept her from getting hurt over and over.

"So, this is the living room," Master Rhodes stated as soon as they were all inside.

Eloise tried not to look at him. Either of them. If she did, she would end up staring and that would be bad.

Master Tiago pointed to the other side of the great room. "Kitchen." He chuckled, probably because those two statements were obvious.

Eloise wandered in farther, drawn toward the sliding glass door that led out to a big backyard. "You have a swing," she murmured as she let her gaze scan the grassy space. "And a sandbox."

"Yep." Master Tiago came up next to her at the doors and set a hand gently on her shoulder. His touch was warm and firm. "We'll go over the house rules with you this afternoon, little one, but one of them will be no leaving the house unless one of us is with you. That means you may not walk out the front door for any reason, but you also may only play in the backyard when one of us can go out with you to supervise."

She glanced at him, breathing heavily. A war of

A CHEERFUL LITTLE COLORING DAY

emotions flitted through her, all in competition with each other.

Part of her wanted to tell him to go fuck himself. The naughtiest, most belligerent side of her was on team "fuck off". She stopped herself from uttering a word to that effect just in time. She'd promised Master Derek she would give this a try. It would be beyond the pale for her to mess it up in less than thirty seconds.

Besides, another side of her was intrigued and excited about the rules these two men might impose on her. She knew from her counseling that she would benefit from structure and rules. Her very Little side needed it.

Eloise believed deep inside she was inherently submissive, but since she'd never met a single Dominant who could control her for very long, she couldn't be certain.

The bottom line was she didn't trust people. They always let her down. And if she let herself care for these two men, it would hurt worse when they, too, let her down.

"Do you want to see the rest of the house, little one?" Master Tiago asked.

"I guess," she muttered. She really wanted to, and they were both being so nice to her, but she was so used to being defiant that it came naturally.

"Come on." Master Rhodes took her hand gently and gave a little tug as he backed up.

Master Tiago grabbed her suitcase from next to the front door and followed behind them.

Master Rhodes pointed out the first room on the left, pushing the door open wider. "Hallway bath. This will be your bathroom."

She glanced inside. It was just a bathroom like any other, but she was secretly kind of excited that she wouldn't have to share it with several other people. "My own?"

"Most of the time, yes. It's also a guest bath, so if

anyone else comes over, they might use it," Master Tiago confirmed.

She continued to stare at it as if it were something special.

Master Tiago set a hand on her shoulder. "We can decorate it if you'd like. It's kinda boring right now. Maybe you like rubber duckies or fish or something?"

She didn't say anything because she felt silly, but what she'd love would be a bathroom that looked like a beach. She'd seen them on television in the commercials.

But this was a temporary arrangement. She couldn't ask them to change the décor of the bathroom, nor would she be presumptuous enough to assume she would be living here for very long. She couldn't possibly be good enough for them to keep her very many days.

It would be easier if she misbehaved now and got it over with fast, but she was too intrigued to blow it yet. She wanted to see more. Perhaps she was making things harder on herself in the long run, but she couldn't help it. Every minute she was in this home was a treat. A blessing.

Master Rhodes stepped halfway into the room across the hallway. "This is an office slash guest room."

She glanced around. Probably she would stay in this room then, right? "Will it be mine for now?" The thought of having her own bathroom was amazing, but the thought of having her own bedroom blew her mind. She'd never ever slept alone in her own room. She hadn't considered that perk when she'd agreed to this.

Master Rhodes frowned. "No, little one. We have a nursery for you." He nodded over his shoulder and kept walking.

Eloise held her breath as she followed him to the room next to the hall bathroom. As soon as she stepped inside, she gasped.

A CHEERFUL LITTLE COLORING DAY

Both men entered with her. Master Tiago set her suitcase down next to the bed. "Again, this room is kind of boring. Like the bathroom. We've never had a Little girl stay with us before, so it's not special. You can think about how you'd like to personalize it."

She could hardly get her feet to move. The carpet was so plush that she felt like she was walking on a cloud. Maybe she was dreaming and she really was walking on air.

Her gaze landed on the daybed first. It had white wrought iron around the sides and against the wall. The bedding was white with fluffy pillows and the thickest comforter she'd ever seen. She wanted to jump onto it and feel it against her cheek.

She shifted her attention to the toybox and the bookshelf next. Both were filled with toys, all kinds of things from dolls to trucks to books and puzzles. It was very gender neutral.

In one corner was a small table and two chairs, just right for her. In another corner was a large rocking chair. All the furniture was white to match the bed. The last item in the room was a changing table. A big one for adult Littles.

She jerked her gaze away from the changing table, too nervous to ask questions about that possibility.

Master Rhodes stepped in front of her and lifted her chin with his fingers. "I see you hesitating about the changing table. Don't panic. We know you enjoy very young age play and spend most of your time in the nursery with the other caterpillars in the Littles' wing, but we also know playing at that age requires a deep level of trust."

Master Tiago set his hand on her lower back. "He's right, little one. For now, we won't pressure you to play that young. You need to get to know us better and develop a more solid relationship with us before we'd expect you to submit to that level in our home."

She swallowed. That was a relief. They both understood. She was certainly attracted to both of them. Who wasn't? But that didn't mean she was instantly ready to let them diaper her and then change her. It would be embarrassing.

It was one thing for Nanny J or Miss Phoebe to change her. She could also tolerate it when other nursery caregivers did, but the thought of these two men she was secretly attracted to openly seeing her private parts made her... Well, the truth was the idea made butterflies jump around inside her. Her panties grew damp.

Yeah, she definitely needed to put her foot down about being diapered by these men. It would be humiliating if they found out she got wet by the idea.

"What do you think, Eloise? Do you like the room?" Master Rhodes asked.

She nodded. "Yes, Sir." For the first time in a while, she couldn't think of a single naughty thing to say. She wasn't feeling disagreeable at the moment. Perhaps she was making a huge mistake in doing so, but they were both being so kind to her.

She knew it couldn't last, but they meant well, and for now she didn't want to burst her bubble. She wouldn't want to ruin things before she had a chance to spend at least one night in this amazing room.

"What's your favorite color, sweet girl?" Master Tiago asked.

She looked up at him. "I don't have one. I like all the colors."

He smiled. "I've seen you coloring a lot at the picnic tables when you're at the park, and Nanny J says you like to color in the nursery too. Is that something you enjoy?"

A CHEERFUL LITTLE COLORING DAY

She nodded. "Coloring is my favorite." Her heart was racing. She felt vulnerable expressing herself. Suddenly, she started to panic from the admission, which made her shake.

Master Rhodes frowned. "What's wrong, little one?"

"Nothing." She shrugged, trying to backpedal. "I mean coloring is fine. It's no big deal."

Master Rhodes's frown grew, his brows coming together. "Well, we got you everything you need to do art." He pointed at the table. "You can sit right over there and color or draw. All the supplies are on the bookshelf."

She glanced at the shelf, noticing the giant box of crayons and another filled with colored pencils. There were coloring books and loose paper too. She wrung her hands together, itching to touch the art supplies. She'd never had her own box of crayons. They looked new.

She couldn't imagine indulging in something so extravagant. This entire idea was a horrible one. She couldn't go through with this. She felt like Annie from the musical. These two men were like her Daddy Warbucks, except there were two of them.

It couldn't last. Nothing ever did. If she let herself get used to having her own room, her own bathroom, and her own crayons, it would hurt so much worse when they grew tired of her.

Overwhelmed, she turned around and ran from the room. She ran back the way she'd come, through the house and straight for the front door. She couldn't breathe in here. She was suffocating.

She had her hand on the doorknob, turning it, when strong arms wrapped around her and pulled her back against a firm chest. "Whatever's gotten into you, sweet girl?" Master Tiago asked. "Where do you think you're going?"

She wiggled in his arms, trying to free herself, but he

25

was much larger and stronger. She didn't stand a chance. "Let me go. This is a terrible idea," she protested. "Take me back to the dorm."

Master Rhodes stepped in front of her and crouched down so his head was slightly lower than hers. "Eloise, we want to help you, but we can't if you don't talk to us."

"You can't help me," she shouted. "This isn't going to work."

"Why not?" he asked as he reached out to stroke her cheek. "We just got here. How can you know that?"

Master Tiago released her just enough to swoop down and lift her off the floor, cradling her in his arms to carry her over to the sofa. He sat, adjusting her on his lap.

Eloise couldn't manage to stop fighting him though. She wiggled and fought to get down. He held both her wrists in one of his large hands and kept his other palm on her hip to keep her from getting free.

Master Rhodes sat next to them, securing her ankles with his hands when she started to kick. "Calm down, little one, before you hurt yourself."

"Let me go."

"Where would you go? It's a bit far to walk back to Rawhide Ranch. And it wouldn't be safe. The roads are curvy. You'd get hit by a car."

"I don't want to stay here," she yelled, working herself up to a full tantrum, though it was hard with both men holding her firmly.

"Give us one good reason why not," Master Tiago demanded.

She continued to squirm, trying in vain to free herself, lips pursed. Nothing about her tantrum was rational. They were right. There was no way she could walk somewhere. But being contrary was part of her, and she didn't know how to be otherwise.

A CHEERFUL LITTLE COLORING DAY

Accepting kindness wasn't something she was capable of. Didn't they understand?

Her hair was wild around her face, and she was exhausted by the time she stopped flailing and sat there panting. Tears started to fall next, infuriating her. She didn't want to cry. She wanted to go back to the Ranch.

Or maybe she should just leave Rawhide Ranch altogether. It was too cushy here. She'd started getting used to a life where there was plenty of food and kind caregivers. She shouldn't let herself get accustomed to this world.

She didn't belong in a place like Rawhide Ranch. Why had she even come here? She should have turned down the offer when it was presented to her and stayed in the shelter where she was living at the time. That was the only life she knew. This one was tempting, taunting her, making her see another way of life.

It wasn't sustainable. No matter how long she stayed, even if she was good and well-behaved, she would never fit in. She didn't even have a high school diploma. The only work she would ever be qualified to do would be cleaning or cooking.

When her breathing finally returned to somewhat normal, Master Tiago spoke in a soft voice. "What was the first rule we told you about when we arrived, sweet girl?"

She hmphed, still trying to tug her hands free.

He didn't let her. "Eloise..." he warned.

She licked her lips. "Not to go out the front door."

"That's right. So, you didn't forget. You were feeling ornery."

She jerked her gaze to his. "I was not," she insisted. "I just don't belong here."

He smiled. "You *do* belong here, sweet girl. You belong here because we invited you, and we're so happy to have you here."

How many times had she heard that line of shit from a foster parent in the past? It usually lasted one day or until the case worker left the house. Some foster parents would say anything while the case worker was dropping her off. She never saw their true colors until no one else was watching.

But no one was watching now. She was alone with two Daddies who were offering her the world. Master Derek may have arranged this, but he wasn't here to see it through. He was back at the Ranch. If Master Rhodes and Master Tiago didn't want to be kind to her, they didn't have to. Not now.

Plus, Master Derek said they had come to him and asked if they could sponsor Eloise. Why would they do that? It wasn't like the real foster system. They weren't getting paid. Were they?

She jerked her gaze to look at them, back and forth. "Is Master Derek paying you to take care of me?"

Master Rhodes's eyes bugged out. "Of course not, little one. That's not how things work here. We volunteered to bring you into our home because we care about you, and we can see you desperately need someone to love you."

She flinched. Love? That was ludicrous. "I'm not lovable," she murmured before she could stop herself.

Master Tiago held her closer. "Of course, you are, sweet girl. You're very lovable, and we're going to prove it to you. It will take time, but we have all the time in the world." He tipped her back in his arms and released her hands to lift her chin. "Look at me, Eloise."

She took a deep breath and met his gaze, pouting.

"You are a precious Little girl who deserves the world. We wouldn't have invited you to move into our home if we didn't think we could build a life with you."

Her mouth fell open. *Build a life with me?*

A CHEERFUL LITTLE COLORING DAY

Master Tiago smiled. "You heard me. We don't want to overwhelm you, but we've been keeping an eye on you for a while. You're a special girl, Eloise, even if you don't know it. Rhodes and I have been looking for our own Little girl for a very long time. We built that nursery, waiting for her. We didn't make this decision flippantly. We want you to be our babygirl, Eloise."

She gasped. Her head was spinning. They couldn't be serious.

Master Rhodes nodded. "We didn't mean to put so much pressure on you so quickly, but it seems like you need to understand how we feel. We didn't invite you here for a week or a month. We desperately hope you will decide to stay for a lifetime."

Eloise couldn't breathe. Her vision swam as she glanced back and forth between them. They were so sincere. Her bottom lip started to tremble. "Don't say things like that," she whispered.

Master Rhodes cupped her face. "Those things are true, and we will say them every day until you believe us."

She stared at him. Tears were forming in the corners of her eyes. He didn't mean to be cruel, but all this talk of a future would be very hurtful in the end.

Two Daddies? She would never even have one Daddy in this lifetime. Not a permanent one anyway. Two? She wouldn't allow herself to believe it was possible.

Master Tiago patted her thighs. "I know it's a lot to consider. We don't even know if you're attracted to either of us. We've put the cart way before the horse here. Do you think you could give us a chance though? Maybe in time you'll come to care for us as much as we already care for you."

Not attracted to them? Was he crazy? Of course she

was attracted to them. She would never tell them that, but she wasn't blind.

Master Rhodes tipped her chin back and met her gaze again. "As much as it pains me to say this, you need to be disciplined for your escape plot, little one. We told you not to walk out the front door, and you openly defied us. We intend to be fair Daddies, but we won't be pushovers. When you break the rules, you will be disciplined."

"There's also the matter of sneaking out of your dorm room last night," Master Tiago added, lifting a brow as he reminded her.

Eloise shuddered. The thought of being spanked by either of these men made her heart race. She liked being spanked. It grounded her. It erased her bad behavior so she could start over with a clean slate. The sting on her bottom was a reminder that someone had paid attention to her.

Master Tiago gently lifted her and turned her so that she was lying across his thighs.

Suddenly she realized the implications of this. Would they pull her pants down? She was wearing a navy cotton dress and matching leggings.

The answer came quickly as Master Tiago pushed her dress up her back before pinning her wrists at the small of her back in one of his hands—much like he'd held her hands in her lap before.

Master Rhodes smoothed his palms up her thighs until he reached the elastic of her leggings and pulled both them and her panties down to her knees.

She whimpered and squirmed, mortified for them to see her bottom. This spanking was nothing like any other spanking she'd received, and there had been many. Too many to count.

Master Derek spanked her several times a week. So did Nanny J and some of the other nursery employees. She was accustomed to having her bottom blistered at least once a day, but this was the first time she would feel the palm of one of these two Daddies she was secretly attracted to.

On top of that, the other one would be watching.

She angled her face so she was staring at the couch cushion, not wanting either man to see the flush or notice how heavily she was breathing.

When Master Rhodes rubbed her bottom with his palm, she sucked in a breath and squeezed her legs together.

Oh no. She tried to wiggle free. This was not like when Master Derek spanked her. This was entirely different.

She shut her eyes tight and willed her body not to react to their touch. Did they realize she was sexually affected by them? If so, they didn't mention it. Thank god. That would increase her mortification tenfold.

She was confused and embarrassed and shaking. She'd sometimes felt this attraction when she was alone and thought about either of these Daddies, but this was different. She was in their home, her bottom naked. She was about to get spanked for being naughty by at least one of the two men she most wanted to spank her.

Master Rhodes slid his palm down to her thighs and held her steady just above her knees.

Master Tiago's hand replaced Master Rhodes's on her butt, rubbing, warming her up, driving her arousal to new heights.

She pursed her lips to keep from reacting.

"I'm going to start slow since you're not used to being spanked by me," Master Tiago informed her. "But I will build up the intensity as I go. I want your bottom to be hot pink for several hours to remind you what happens when Little girls are naughty in this house."

She whimpered through her clenched teeth.

Master Tiago lifted his palm and brought it back down in a gentle swat.

She released her breath when it didn't hurt but then sucked it back in as he continued. He didn't give her much time to recuperate after each spank. His palm moved around to cover every inch of her skin, the pressure gradually increasing.

It burned exactly how she liked it. Her entire butt and the backs of her thighs stung. If the two of them hadn't been holding her so firmly, she would have fought them to wiggle free. Not from the spanking. That part was so good. But she really didn't want them to find out her pussy was soaking wet and needy.

By the time Master Tiago was done, she was crying. She hadn't even realized she was sobbing until he smoothed his palm over her heated skin and cooed to her softly. "That's a good girl. Let it out."

Her butt was on fire. Probably worse than any time Master Derek had swatted her. But her pussy was on fire too. With a strange raw need that confused her.

Master Rhodes rubbed her thighs. "We're so proud of you, little one." He finally eased her panties and leggings back over her butt before Master Tiago rolled her over and cradled her in his arms.

She winced. Her butt hurt. It was still confusing. Intellectually, she knew from the other Littles and from her counselor that lots of people enjoyed a thorough spanking, but this was the first time it had been so euphoric for her.

Master Tiago held her close and rocked her in his arms. He took a tissue from Master Rhodes and wiped her face before holding it to her nose. "Blow, sweet girl."

She obeyed him but the act of kindness only made her cry harder. She cried for a long time, unable to stop, a full

A CHEERFUL LITTLE COLORING DAY

ugly cry that seemed to come out of nowhere and wouldn't go away.

After a long time, she finally sniffled back the last of her tears, exhausted and unable to face these two Daddies. All she could do was turn her face toward Master Tiago's chest and squeeze her eyes closed.

"Feel better, little one?" Master Rhodes asked, his hand on her thigh again. He'd maintained contact with her the entire time so that it felt like both men were participating in her punishment.

She whimpered, uncertain how to respond.

When Master Tiago suddenly stood, holding her against his chest, she wrapped her small arms around him and held on tight. He kissed her forehead. "I bet you could use a nap, huh, sweet girl?"

She sniffled. She was indeed exhausted. Mentally and physically drained. She hadn't gotten enough sleep last night, and this morning had been challenging so far.

She was aware of Master Rhodes taking the lead and entering the nursery in front of them. He pulled the covers back on the daybed so Master Tiago could lower her to the mattress.

They each removed one of her tennis shoes before pulling the covers up over her and tucking them around her.

Eloise was trembling from the spanking and the attention.

"Do you have a special stuffie in your suitcase, sweet girl?" Master Tiago asked.

She nodded. "Peaches," she murmured.

Master Rhodes opened the suitcase at the foot of the bed and seconds later held up her bunny.

She smiled as she took the stuffie from him and pulled Peaches under the covers. "Thank you." She knew she was smiling, and being polite wasn't really in her bag of tricks, but at the moment, all she could do was accept their kindness and return it.

"Nap, little one," Master Rhodes stated as he leaned over and kissed her forehead in the same spot Master Tiago had moments ago.

She couldn't remember a single time when anyone had kissed her like that. If they had when she was young, it didn't stand out in her mind. It felt so very nice. She could get used to it.

But she shouldn't. Eventually, this would all end, and then she'd have the memories to make her feel even worse than she did now.

Already she was piling up memories. It was a dangerous slippery slope. The intense spanking. Her wet panties. The way they held her and stroked her skin. The kisses.

She needed to shove those memories aside and protect herself. If not, she would be doomed to a life of unhappiness.

CHAPTER FOUR

"Maybe we should have installed a monitor in her room," Rhodes said as he paced the kitchen.

Tiago shook his head where he was leaning against the counter. "We need to discuss that with her first. It would have been a violation of her privacy if we'd done it without her knowledge."

Rhodes sighed. Tiago was right. "I hate that she's on the floor in there. Why would she move to the floor?" She must have moved to the floor as soon as they'd left the room because that's where he'd found her curled up the first time he'd peeked into her nursery.

Tiago shrugged. "Maybe she didn't like the bed. Maybe the mattress is too soft or too hard. We'll figure it out and fix it when she wakes up."

Rhodes ran a hand over his face. He was so frustrated. He wanted to make her life easier, not harder. They both did. She was so reluctant to let anyone past her walls, but he and Tiago were determined to do so. They would eventually succeed. At least he hoped and prayed they would.

"What if she doesn't feel the same way about us that we feel about her?" Rhodes asked.

"Then we let her go." Tiago shoved off the counter and opened the fridge to grab a bottle of water. "But it's way too soon to know that. She needs time. I don't think anyone has loved her. It makes her leery and unable to trust."

"It makes my heart hurt," Rhodes muttered.

"You need to get some sleep. You were up all night, and you have to work again tonight."

"There's no way I could sleep right now. My adrenaline is pumping too hard. Maybe we should check on her again." He spun around, intent on peeking in her room again, but stopped short.

Eloise was standing in the hallway at the entrance to the great room. She had her bunny in her arms and her thumb in her mouth. Her gorgeous black hair was a tussled mess, the pigtails having slipped down so that tendrils escaped on both sides.

She was still half asleep and she'd never been more adorable.

Rhodes's heart nearly stopped at the sight of her. She'd captivated his attention months ago, but now that he had her in his home, he would finally get to see sides of her he hadn't ever been privy to before. Starting with this one. Sleepy Eloise.

"Hey, babygirl." He rushed toward her and scooped her off the floor before he could think to stop himself from overwhelming her. Luckily, she didn't balk. She released her thumb and laid her head on his shoulder.

Rhodes carried her to the island and set her on top, keeping his hands around her so she wouldn't fall. "Did you have a nice nap, little one?" he asked as he smoothed a lock of hair from her face.

A CHEERFUL LITTLE COLORING DAY

She nodded.

Tiago came to her side. "Why were you sleeping on the floor, sweet girl?"

She shrugged.

"Is the bed too soft or too hard? We can get a different mattress," Tiago continued, pressing her for details.

She shook her head. Damn she was fucking adorable. It was like she hadn't yet woken up enough to remember she preferred to be angry. This side of Eloise was sweet and precious. "It's fine," she murmured.

Rhodes rubbed her back. "Did you fall off?" This had been a concern of his ever since he first found her on the floor next to the bed. He'd nearly run in to make sure she was okay, but Tiago had stopped him, pointing out she was curled up with her bunny and her pillow. She was fine. She'd gotten out of bed intentionally and moved to the floor. The question was, why?

She shook her head again. "No."

A knot formed in Rhodes's throat. "Eloise, tell Daddy why you were on the floor."

She tipped her pretty face back to meet his gaze, probably startled by him referring to himself as Daddy. But damn, he wanted to be her Daddy so badly it hurt. The sooner she started calling him that, the sooner his heart would unclench.

Her voice was almost too soft to hear, but she finally answered their question. "It was too perfect. I didn't want to get used to it."

That tightness in his chest doubled, and he saw Tiago's face twitch and his jaw stiffen at the same time.

Rhodes decided the best way to handle her would be to make rules and be firm about them. "From now on, when we put you in your bed, you'll stay there, understood?"

She blinked at him, hugging her bunny closer to her chest.

"I'm going to install a monitor in the corner of your room this afternoon, sweet girl," Tiago informed her. "That way you'll be able to call out and let us know if you need us when you're in your bed."

"I can just get up and come find you," she informed them.

Rhodes shook his head. "Little girls need to stay in their beds at night and during naps. We'll put up a side rail when you're in bed. It will keep you safe."

She stared at him, her lip quivering. Finally, she whispered, "Okay."

She was hard to read. Most of the time he felt like she was thinking of anything she could come up with to be contrary. Sometimes, she simply gave in. It would seem she might be softer and more pliable when she was tired or had recently woken up.

"I bet you're hungry," Tiago said, patting her back. "We don't want to overwhelm you with too many choices, but we also don't want to be presumptuous on your first day. Would you prefer to take a bottle right now or eat Big-girl food from a plate?"

She chewed on her bottom lip, contemplating. In the end, she sighed and said, "I'll eat regular food." Her shoulders sank at the same time as if that wasn't the answer she wanted to give, but she'd forced herself to make that choice for some reason.

"Eloise..." Rhodes encouraged. "Look at me."

She shifted her attention to him. "Please don't tell us what you think we want to hear. If we ask you a question, we expect an honest answer." He lifted a brow.

Her cheeks flushed, and she swallowed, but she repeated the same answer. "I'd like to eat real food, Sir."

He didn't think she was being sincere for some reason, though he had no idea why. He would take her word for it this time and not pressure her further.

"Okay then." Tiago turned toward the fridge and pulled out the makings for sandwiches. "Rhodes and I were just about to make lunch, so your timing is perfect. Do you like sandwiches, sweet girl?"

She nodded. "Yes, Sir."

"What do you like on them?" he asked.

Rhodes kept his hands on her, one on her thigh and one at her side. He told himself it was to make sure she didn't fall, but the truth was he didn't want to break the connection. Eloise was soft and agreeable right now, and that was a blessing.

"I don't care," she murmured.

Tiago froze and looked at her. "Of course you care, sweet girl. Everyone cares what they have on their sandwich."

She shook her head, her hair flipping around. "I'll eat whatever you make, Master Tiago."

Tiago visibly stiffened. "Let me rephrase. If you were in the cafeteria line making a sandwich, what would you put on it?"

She glanced at the items on the counter and then back at him. "Peanut butter and jelly."

Rhodes chuckled. Neither of those items were on the counter, so she'd probably felt like she shouldn't choose them. "Peanut butter and jelly it is," he declared as he leaned in to kiss her temple. He loved standing this close to her, inhaling her sweet scent, feeling her pulse.

Tiago grinned and headed for the pantry. "I can do that. Do you want white bread or wheat?"

She glanced at the counter again.

Rhodes lifted his hand from her thighs to cover her

eyes playfully. "Don't look at what's out. Just tell Tiago what you'd prefer."

She gasped against his palm, but responded. "White."

Tiago headed for the pantry again and returned with white bread. Thank goodness they'd had some. "Crusts or no crusts?" he asked next.

She gasped. "That would be wasteful."

Rhodes drew in a deep breath, cupped her face, and looked her in the eye. "Cutting off your crusts is not a giant waste, little one. If that's how you prefer your sandwich, that's how we will prepare it."

"Okay."

This precious Little girl had suffered from food insecurity in the past. The signs were all there. Maybe no one else had noticed in the cafeteria. He would bet she was very careful to only choose what she wanted and clean her plate. He'd seen food insecurity before. It broke his heart.

Tiago prepared her sandwich, cut it in triangles, and arranged it on a plate. "Apples? Carrots?"

"Okay."

Tiago shook his head. "Not okay. Tell me what you'd like. Do you like apples and carrots?"

"I like apples," she said.

"Perfect. Can I cut them in wedges and maybe sprinkle cinnamon on them?"

She smiled. Blessed angels. "Yes, Sir."

Rhodes refused to get his hopes up, but this new Little girl who'd awoken from her nap was far more agreeable than the one who'd first walked in the front door this morning.

Rhodes wrapped his arms around Eloise and slid her off the island to settle her in the highchair.

She sucked in a breath as she realized where she was seated.

A CHEERFUL LITTLE COLORING DAY

"Arms up, babygirl. Let Daddy buckle you in." He knew he was pushing it by referring to himself as Daddy. It was too soon. Way too soon. But damn she was so sweet and soft right now. And he wanted her to be his Little girl so badly he could taste it.

Luckily, Eloise lifted her arms and let him bring the strap across her waist and between her legs. He fastened her in, tightened the sides, and attached the tray. "There we go. Now you won't fall." He tapped her nose, his chest tightening again. She was almost smiling.

Tiago slid a plate in front of her. "How's this, sweet girl?" he asked. "Everything to your liking?"

She definitely smiled this time. "Yes, Sir." And then she used both hands to pick up her sandwich and bring it to her mouth. Precious.

Tiago made turkey and provolone for the two men, adding cut up apples since he was already doing so. They sat on tall stools at the island on either side of Eloise.

Rhodes glanced at Tiago and then addressed her. "We want you to know that your age preference doesn't affect how we feel about you in the least. Even though you've played at a young age for a while, you're not required to stick with that. We'll watch you for clues and talk about it often to help guide you into whatever age you're most comfortable with." He reached over and set his hand on top of hers for a moment before letting go.

"Okay," she muttered, not looking up.

Tiago finished chewing and swallowing a bite before adding, "Rhodes needs to sleep after lunch. He's been up since last night. I took today off so I can be with you this afternoon, but after today, we'll tag team you most of the time."

She lifted her gaze, looking confused.

Tiago grinned. "Bonus of having two Daddies who work different shifts is that you'll never be alone."

"You're not really my Daddies," she mumbled. "I know you're trying to help me, but you don't have to do that."

"Do what? Think of you as our Little girl?" Rhodes asked. "Too late. We're already wrapped around your pinkies. One on each hand. You're welcome to call us Master Rhodes and Master Tiago for as long as you'd like. Sir is fine too. But you're also permitted to call us Daddy and Papa whenever you're ready."

Eloise picked up her sippy cup of milk and gulped down a huge drink before setting the cup down with shaky fingers. "Don't do that," she whispered.

"Do what, sweet girl?" Tiago asked.

Rhodes could feel her sweet, fresh-from-a-nap self slipping away. "Ask me to pretend this is real. It's mean."

She'd finished her sandwich, so Rhodes dragged her highchair around to face him. He looked her in the eye and cleared his throat. "This *is* real, babygirl. For me it's real. For Tiago it's real. Like I said earlier, we didn't invite you here for a trial. We've known for a long time that we wanted to approach you. It was time. We care about you. Deeply."

She stared at him.

Tiago rose and came to Rhodes's side to face her head on. "He's right, sweet girl. I know it's going to take time for you to believe us and trust us, but we have nothing but time. We're here for the long haul. However long it takes. Days, weeks, months, it's up to you. When you're ready to believe us, we'll be ready to accept you with open arms."

She rolled her eyes. Yeah, the other Eloise was back. "Can I get down now?"

Rhodes lifted a brow. It was hard not to chuckle at her total insubordination, but he didn't want her to think for

A CHEERFUL LITTLE COLORING DAY

one second he was making fun of her. "How about if you ask in a nicer way, little one."

She sighed. "May I please get down, Sir?" Her voice was surly and filled with fake exasperation.

Tiago cleared his throat. "Let's try that one more time."

She crossed her arms and hmphed, staring at her tray.

Tiago reached for Rhodes's plate and started clearing the island from their lunches.

Rhodes joined him, wiping down the counter and then cleaning off Eloise's tray before taking the risk to wipe her face and hands.

She let him but then went right back to pouting, arms crossed.

Without a word, both men grabbed their laptops, settled at the island, and went to work.

Rhodes couldn't be sure what Tiago was doing on his, but Rhodes was pretending to read emails. He figured Tiago was doing something similar. Looking busy. Acting like they didn't care if their Little girl was having a silent tantrum.

She was definitely ornery and unpredictable. It was clear that her intention was to sabotage this relationship so she wouldn't get hurt, and Rhodes could understand that. It made perfect sense given her history.

Eloise wasn't going to win this battle or this war though.

Rhodes glanced up at Tiago without lifting his head to find his friend fighting a wry smile. They were on the same page. They could and would wait her out. Today and then again every day. Until she believed they cared about her.

She was worth it. Rhodes knew deep inside was a precious Little girl who was hurting. She deserved a break. She deserved a forever.

CHAPTER FIVE

Eloise hated being ignored. It was almost worse than being spanked. No. It was a lot worse. The spanking had been kind of nice. At least when she was being punished, people were paying attention to her. It beat being ignored by a mile.

This was her fault. She knew it. But now that she'd dug her heels in, it was hard to alter her course.

Neither man glanced at her a single time. They were intently working on their computers as if she weren't even in the room. It was infuriating.

Eventually, she needed to pee.

She squeezed her thighs together tightly and tried to ignore her bladder for a while, but finally, she started doing a potty dance in her chair. "I need to use the bathroom," she muttered.

Master Rhodes glanced at her. "I bet you do. Maybe if you ask politely, one of us will release the tray and unbuckle you so you can get down."

"I can do it myself, you know," she countered defensively.

"Yep. But you won't." Master Rhodes went back to his computer.

Eloise was angry now. "It's not healthy for girls to hold their peepee," she blurted. *Don't they know anything?*

Master Tiago turned to face her this time. "You're right, sweet girl. It can cause a UTI. You should probably go use the bathroom. Neither of us is preventing you from doing so. *You* are the one too stubborn to go potty."

"I could wet my pants right here. Then you'd have to clean it up," she tossed back. It was becoming difficult to come up with more ways to be argumentative.

"Also true," Master Tiago agreed. "We'll take that to mean you would prefer to be diapered, and that doesn't bother me at all. Does it bother you, Rhodes?"

Master Rhodes shook his head. "Nope." He smiled at her. *Smiled.* Darn him. "I assume you're most suited for younger age play, babygirl. If you want to move in that direction today, that's fine with us. If you want to be diapered, all you have to do is ask. Or, wet your pants. I'll take that as a silent plea."

Ugh. She wasn't getting anywhere. They had an answer for everything. Maddening. She considered her options. They obviously knew her well. She did enjoy younger age play, but she didn't think she would like it all the time.

Sometimes, it was nice to be taken care of and pampered. The only times she was able to let her mind fully relax was when she didn't have to worry about anything at all. That was why she liked spending time in the Caterpillar Room at least for a few hours every day. She felt the most authentic there.

But these two Daddies didn't know her that well yet. They were speculating. And she wasn't ready for them to spread her legs and touch her private parts yet. Was she?

She really, really needed to pee now. It was time to end

A CHEERFUL LITTLE COLORING DAY

this particular charade. If she got any more defiant by trying to remove her own tray and unbuckle herself, she would probably end up over one of their knees again. Her bottom still stung from being spanked earlier.

Taking a deep breath, she found the will to be polite. "May I please get down from the highchair so I can go potty, Sir?" It didn't matter which Sir she was referring to.

Master Rhodes pushed away from the island and came to her. "What a nice Little girl. See? Easy."

She pursed her lips to keep from responding with something snarky while he removed her tray and unfastened her buckle. He also lifted her to the floor.

As soon as she was free, she took off running toward the bathroom. She shut the door and hurried to pull down her leggings before she really did have an accident.

After using the toilet, she washed her hands and dried them on the pretty white towel before exiting the bathroom. Now what? Should she return to the kitchen?

"Come here, Eloise," Master Tiago requested.

Apparently so.

She tried really hard to stuff her defiant attitude down deep as she shuffled back into the great room.

Master Rhodes was standing next to the island, shutting his computer. "I need to sleep for a while, Little one. I have to work third shift again tonight. Tiago is going to take you out back."

She glanced at the door. That sounded amazing. "Okay," she murmured, not wanting either man to know how much she liked their plan.

Master Rhodes came toward her, tipped her head back with his fingers under her chin, and met her gaze. He didn't look the least bit angry with her. After the way she'd behaved for the last half hour, she expected exasperation, but this man seemed to have a bottomless well of patience.

"I care about you, Eloise. Master Tiago does too." He stroked her cheek. "Try to enjoy yourself. It will be much more fun than fighting us at every turn. I promise."

When he leaned over and kissed her forehead, she drew in a breath. It felt so good. She loved it when they kissed her face. Anywhere. It brought them close. She could smell his aftershave, or maybe it was his shampoo. It didn't matter. It smelled manly and made her shiver a bit.

Master Rhodes released her before heading down the hallway.

She turned around to watch him. When they'd given her a tour earlier, they hadn't made it past the nursery. There were two more rooms at the end of the hall. Since Master Rhodes entered the one on the left, she assumed the one on the right was Master Tiago's room.

She jumped when Master Tiago set his hands on her shoulders. She hadn't noticed him approaching. He leaned over her. "Sorry, sweet girl. I didn't mean to startle you. Would you like to go out back?"

She nodded.

He released her shoulders but took her hand in his. "Let's get your shoes, and how about if I fix your pigtails? They got messy during your nap."

"Okay." She let him lead her back to her nursery where he lifted her up and set her on the edge of the bed. He squatted down in front of her and picked up one shoe, loosening the shoestrings before reaching for her foot.

"I can do that," she protested. *Why must I be so contrary? Let the man put your shoes on.*

"I'm sure you can, sweet girl, but I would enjoy doing it for you. Is that okay?" He waited for her to respond.

She finally lifted her foot out and he slid her shoe on. While he tied it, he said, "I haven't had a Little girl in my house for many years, Eloise. It's a pleasure having you

A CHEERFUL LITTLE COLORING DAY

here. I'm so excited to be your caregiver. I hope you'll let me do little things for you. It brings me joy."

She bit her lip while she watched him put her other shoe on. The butterflies danced in her tummy again. She couldn't remember a time when someone put her shoes on. Even though she spent time in the nursery most days, she always arrived already dressed with her shoes on and laces tied.

Living at Rawhide Ranch had so many perks but being a Little without a Daddy had a lot of downfalls. One of them was missing out on this kind of individual attention. A Little without a Daddy couldn't be Little fulltime. It wasn't possible. She had to do things for herself.

When Master Tiago was done, he stood, helped her down from the bed, and once again held her hand to lead her into the bathroom.

She watched as he opened a drawer, found a brush, and angled her to face the mirror. He carefully removed one of her hairbands before brushing out her thick hair, gathering it up high on her head, and replacing the rubber band.

In minutes, he had the other one also fixed. They were better than she could do herself, and she smiled at her reflection before she could stop herself.

"Would you like some ribbons, sweet girl?" he asked.

"You have ribbons?" She definitely wanted ribbons. She wanted to stay right here in this small bathroom for as long as she could with this doting Daddy. Maybe it was a horrible idea that would endear her to him even more, but she was enjoying his attention.

"How about these?" Mater Tiago pulled two navy ribbons from a drawer that was filled with ribbons of all colors.

"Wow." She peered inside. "That's a lot of ribbons."

"Yep. No matter what you're wearing, we should be able

to find something to match." He carefully tied them in her hair and then met her gaze in the mirror. "You're so pretty, sweet girl. You take my breath away."

Was he serious? Except for Master Rhodes, no one ever told her she was pretty. Probably to most people she wasn't because she was always scowling.

When he bent down to kiss the top of her head, she closed her eyes, enjoying the feel of him so close to her. His hands were on her shoulders, his lips on her head, his body inches from her back. It felt nice. Too nice. It scared her.

"Ready to go outside?"

"Yes, Sir."

When they reached the sliding glass door, Master Tiago reached up to the very top and unlatched the lock. It was above her head. She would need a chair to get this door open. That was intentional. She wasn't supposed to go outside alone. It was one of the rules.

As soon as they stepped outside, Master Tiago nodded toward the yard. "Would you like me to push you on the swing? Or we could build a sandcastle. Master Rhodes said you like sand."

"No, thank you. I'll just play by myself." She hated herself the moment those words came out of her mouth. *Why do I always say the wrong things?*

It would be much more fun if Master Tiago played with her. Playing alone was boring. It was also safe. No one could hurt her if she was alone. And, she couldn't hurt them either. Not that she would physically hurt anyone. She would never do that. But she could be verbally mean to people. She did that often. It was like she couldn't stop herself.

Feeling sorry for herself, Eloise trudged over to the sandbox. There were several bright plastic toys inside, including a shovel and several buckets. She sat on the edge

A CHEERFUL LITTLE COLORING DAY

of the sandbox and stared at them, toeing the sand with her tennis shoe. She didn't feel like playing. Not alone. Instead, she sat there staring at nothing, thinking about her choices.

Not just the choice she had at the moment but all her options. Every time she opened her mouth, she made choices. Some were good. Some were horrible. More often than not, she made bad choices. It was easier to be naughty than good.

She didn't have friends. Not really. She'd never had any. When she'd been young, she'd often moved from one school to the next as she was sent to different foster homes. She rarely stayed in one place long enough to make friends. Plus, no one ever invited a foster kid to come play at their house.

Those were the years when she started getting sad and later mad. She misbehaved because it made people notice her. It also got her into trouble and caused her problems.

Now, she was a grown adult. She didn't have to continue this path of destruction. She could change. Be kind. Smile. Make friends. Would any of the Little girls who lived at the Ranch even want to be her friend after all the times she was mean to them?

Eloise wasn't certain she was even capable of changing. She didn't know how to be consistently good. She should try. For Master Rhodes and Master Tiago. They were so nice and patient. How long would they continue to indulge her if she kept pushing them away?

CHAPTER SIX

Tiago felt restless as he watched Eloise sit on the edge of the sandbox. She didn't touch the toys. She seemed to be staring at nothing. Thinking.

He let her be for a long time, hoping she was processing her new environment. He wanted the world for her. He knew Rhodes did too. They'd discussed it many times in the past few months. The pretty Little girl with the raven hair and big blue eyes.

They'd watched her from afar, noticing how sad she was. Lonely. Distressed. It was obvious to anyone who paid attention that all Eloise wanted was to be loved.

After a while, Tiago decided to intervene in her pity party. He couldn't stand to watch her sit there any longer. "Eloise? Why don't you come sit with me on the porch swing?"

She jerked her head his direction. For a moment he suspected she'd been so far in her head she'd forgotten where she was. "That's okay," she finally said. "I'm fine."

"It's kind of lonely over here. If you change your mind,

I'd love for you to sit with me." He wouldn't force her, but the ache he felt in his chest was real.

Eloise was his Little girl. He'd known for a while. She was also Rhodes's. The two of them had confessed their attraction to her one day and chuckled about their mutual affection for the same Little.

It had been convenient since they lived together. It would be so much easier if they found a Little girl who wouldn't mind sharing two Daddies. Eloise was the perfect person to make their home complete. She needed more care than other Littles, and with two of them, they could provide it.

Chances were she would always need reassurance and encouragement. Tiago was up to the task, and he knew Rhodes was too.

When Rhodes came home this morning and told Tiago what had happened in the night, it had been a no-brainer. It was time to meet with Master Derek, express their concerns, propose this arrangement.

There were no guarantees. Tiago felt confident he and Rhodes could get Eloise to come out of her shell and learn to enjoy life over time, but what he didn't know for sure was if she was interested in them as more than simple caregivers.

It was too soon to bring that subject up, but Tiago was more and more certain with every passing hour today that he wanted this Little girl to be his in every way. He'd seen glimpses of the real Eloise several times. Those big blue eyes could bring any man to his knees.

Everything about her called to him. She was stunningly gorgeous. Every inch of her. Her Little was precious beyond belief. On the rare moments when she smiled, it lit up her face. Her full pouty lips made him hard every time she licked them.

A CHEERFUL LITTLE COLORING DAY

He wouldn't scare her off by telling her how he felt. She deserved better. Baby steps. First and foremost, he and Rhodes needed to get her to open up, trust them to care for her, and believe in herself. If they could accomplish that much, maybe she would learn to see them as more.

If she didn't...

Nope. Tiago couldn't face that possibility. It hurt.

He continued to watch her as she did nothing but drag her tennis shoes through the sand. *Please, Eloise. Come to me.* He willed her to accept his offer, but he had to wait for her. Let her make her own decisions.

Finally, after a long silence, she seemed to take a deep breath as she turned to face him. She held his gaze for a moment and then pushed to standing and shuffled toward him. "I'd like to sit with you now, Sir," she whispered.

He scooted to one side of the porch swing. "I'd like that, sweet girl." He took her hand to help her climb up, and when she settled several inches from him, he closed the distance, draping his arm behind her on the back of the swing.

She stared at her lap, fidgeting her hands for a few minutes, but finally she silently leaned into him, setting her head on his shoulder.

Tiago closed his eyes and inhaled slowly. He wanted to shout for joy at this small victory, but he didn't want to startle her, so he settled for lowering his arm down around her shoulders and holding her against his side.

He pushed the swing in an easy rhythm. He wanted more from her. He wanted the world. But this victory tasted so good, he didn't want to rock the boat.

After a while, she surprised him by tipping her head back to meet his gaze. "Why did you ask me to come stay with you?" Her question was so earnest. So raw.

Tiago swallowed. His response was important. He also

didn't want to lie to her. "You caught my attention a while ago, sweet girl. Mine and Rhodes. We've been hoping a day might come when you would be willing to give us a chance."

"A chance for what?" Her eyes were wide and innocent. She really wanted to know the score here. "I don't want to be a charity case."

He sucked in a breath and squeezed her shoulders. "You will never be a charity case, Eloise. I don't see you that way."

"What way do you see me? As a Little girl?"

"I do see your Little girl. I see how sad your Little is and how badly she could use a Daddy. Or how about two Daddies? But I also see your adult in there." He reached over with his other hand to tap her temple. "Inside your mind and heart is an amazing woman who captured my attention and hasn't let it go."

She sucked in a surprised breath and then went silent again for a while. When she lifted her feet and tucked them to her side, he eased her down onto the bench of the swing so she rested her head in his lap.

She was exhausted. Anyone could see that. More from the stress of the constant energy she spent every day trying to be combative than anything else.

Tiago wanted to see her relax, let out her breath, lower her shoulders. He wanted her to have a soft place to fall and be able to trust that he and Rhodes would provide that.

It was going to take time, but it turned out he had all the time in the world for this Little girl. The first steps had finally taken place. She was in their home, under their roof. She would always have food and clothes and shelter. Now, they just needed to convince her those things would never be taken away.

The other thing she needed, perhaps more than meals,

A CHEERFUL LITTLE COLORING DAY

dresses, and a bedroom, was love. She deserved to be loved unconditionally and never have that taken away either. How long would it take for her to believe she deserved and would have their love? Even if it took a lifetime, he would wait.

"I don't know how to be someone's Little girl," she confessed softly.

Tiago stroked his hand up and down her arm, her hip, her thigh. Over and over, hoping his touch would calm her. "It will come naturally, sweet girl."

"Why do you call me sweet girl?" she asked his lap. "I'm not sweet at all."

He swallowed. "Of course you are. The sweetest Little girl ever. She's inside you. Sometimes she pokes her head out to look around. She's skittish and nervous. I understand that. We both do. Eventually, Eloise Grace will find her true self deep inside and settle into her. I promise."

She frowned as she curled her arms up against her chest. "What if you're wrong?"

"I'm not. Daddies know these things. You do too. I bet when you're quiet and alone, you know there's a sweet, loving, precious Little girl inside you who's desperate to come out and stay. She peeks out sometimes, but she's scared. The world hasn't been kind to her. People have hurt her over and over. It's hard to trust that we won't be like them. But I promise we will not let you down."

She rolled onto her back so she could stare up at him. "How do you know so much about me?"

"Observation. You're not the first Little girl to come to Rawhide Ranch with baggage, sweet girl. Everyone has baggage, but some people have been forced to carry more than their share. I know you have. I can see it in your eyes."

She pursed her lips, blinking at him.

He set his hand over hers on her tummy and threaded

their fingers together, hoping it would help her feel cocooned. Cared for. "I'd bet my last dollar that the reason you break rules and misbehave goes much deeper than wanting attention. I bet you do those things to test the people around you. To prove that no one wants you by forcing them to turn their backs on you." He lifted a brow and let her ponder that.

She stared at him, her lips parted.

He was reaching her. Thank god. So, he continued, "It's easier to get people to push you away sooner rather than later before you start to care about them, isn't it, sweet girl?"

She sniffled and rolled back onto her side. She let Tiago keep his hand threaded with hers though, and she absently brought her other hand up to her mouth to suck her thumb. He doubted she knew she was doing it.

Tiago wanted the world for this Little girl. He wanted to speed up time to get to a place where she was happy and well-adjusted and living in her authentic skin.

Time. Darn time held up everything.

CHAPTER SEVEN

"Why are your fingers all blue, babygirl?" Master Rhodes asked Eloise as he lifted her hand to kiss the tips of her fingers. "Did you get blue marker on them?" he teased.

She was sitting in her highchair coloring while Master Tiago cooked dinner. Master Rhodes had just emerged from sleeping.

She shook her head, grinning at him. "Master Tiago gave me a popsicle. It ran all down my fingers because I couldn't eat it fast enough."

"Ah. Then I bet these fingers are tasty." Master Rhodes sucked two of them into his mouth, drawing them deep before letting them out with a pop.

Eloise's heart nearly stopped. The gesture was so erotic.

"Bleh," he said. "I guess Papa also washed them afterward. The dye seeped in, but you taste like soap."

She giggled before she could stop herself.

He smiled so wide, his eyes dancing. "I love that sound, babygirl." He released her hand, cupped her neck, and kissed her forehead. "What did you two do all day? Besides eat popsicles of course."

Eloise tipped her head back and looked up at her handsome... Daddy? "Do Little girls call you Daddy and Master Tiago Papa?"

He shook his head. "Nope. Little girls call us Master Rhodes and Master Tiago. The only one who will call us Daddy and Papa is you." He tapped her nose.

She blinked. "Oh."

He smiled again. "What's Papa making for dinner?"

She set her crayon down. "Pasghetti."

"Is that so?" He chuckled. "Did you choose that meal?"

She nodded. "He said maybe if I get red sauce all over my fingers, they will turn purple."

Another deep chuckle barreled out of him. He'd said he liked the sound of her laughter. She liked his too. "I guess we better find you a bib before you eat so you don't get pasghetti on your dress."

"Okay." She tipped her head back to the page she was coloring as Master Rhodes... Daddy... headed for the refrigerator. She felt like she was in a dream. Or she'd slipped into another dimension. She'd been here less than a day and her world was completely different.

Instead of getting in line in the cafeteria with the other Littles at Rawhide Ranch tonight, she was sitting in this kitchen with two Daddies doting on her. It was out of body. Unexpected. Unsettling.

She'd been good all afternoon for... Papa. Even letting that word slip into her head was difficult. She shouldn't think of them as her Daddies. They weren't, not really. They were sponsoring her. They would only keep her until she misbehaved so badly they didn't want her anymore.

Except both of them had made it clear they would not send her back. She shouldn't trust them. She wouldn't let herself. No one had ever kept her. Why would Master Rhodes and Master Tiago? Daddy and Papa. Two Daddies.

A CHEERFUL LITTLE COLORING DAY

No one got to have two amazing Daddies, especially not a naughty girl like her.

"Hey there, little one." Daddy set his hand on top of hers, stilling her coloring.

When she glanced at the page, she noticed she'd been viciously scribbling all over the paper, ruining her picture. She hadn't even realized it.

"Are you okay, sweet girl?" Papa asked.

Suddenly, their kind tones got under her skin. She felt like this was all a joke. Someone was going to start laughing at her any moment. Maybe she was dreaming, and she would wake up and realize none of this had happened.

Eloise picked up a handful of crayons and threw them across the room. They scattered all over the floor.

Daddy... was he really her Daddy? Master Rhodes... grabbed the sides of her highchair and bent down so he was at eye level. "What brought that on, babygirl?" he asked in a very calm voice.

She crossed her arms and furrowed her brow, easily slipping back into her naughty skin. It was safer there. If she didn't let anyone be kind to her, she wouldn't get hurt.

She'd let herself be vulnerable today. Now she was going to remember this day forever and feel sad. She never should have let her guard down. It would hurt worse later.

"We don't throw our crayons, little one," Master Rhodes informed her.

She glared at him. "That's not a rule."

He lifted both brows.

Master Tiago chuckled behind her as he joined them. "Technically, she's right. We didn't go over the rest of the house rules." He narrowed his gaze when he got in her line of sight though. "However, you know better. That's not appropriate behavior for anywhere at any time."

He collected the rest of the crayons off her tray and the

coloring book. When he turned around, she watched him, holding her breath as he put them up high on a shelf in the cabinet.

Uh oh. Throwing crayons hadn't probably been her best choice considering she probably wouldn't see them again for a long time and coloring was her favorite activity.

Master Tiago spoke again as he returned. "The coloring book and crayons can stay in time out for a while since a certain Little girl doesn't appreciate them." He wasn't angry. He never raised his voice. He was just stating facts.

Eloise wanted to cry. *Why did I do that?*

Master Rhodes unfastened her highchair tray and the buckles at her waist before lifting her into his arms. He carried her to the couch as if she were about to receive a present instead of get her butt spanked.

Emotions overwhelmed her. She was used to being spanked. Master Derek spanked her often. He never lost his cool either. None of the caregivers did at Rawhide Ranch. But this was different. For the first time Eloise could remember, she felt remorseful.

She didn't like the idea that she'd misbehaved with these two kind Daddies. A part of her wanted to take it back. She wanted to be good for them.

Being good wasn't something she was proficient at, however. She didn't know how. She'd been a nice girl for a long time today, but it felt like she was in someone else's skin. Eloise didn't even know that girl.

When Master Rhodes sat on the couch, he stood her up in front of him between his legs. His hands were on her hips. They were eye to eye.

As he held her gaze, she started to cry. Silent tears that rolled down her cheeks.

Master Rhodes lifted his hands to her face and swiped them away with his thumbs. "I know you're going through a

A CHEERFUL LITTLE COLORING DAY

transition, babygirl. We understand. It's hard to move to a new environment. I'm sure a million thoughts are going through your head right now."

She swallowed, trying not to cry harder. She didn't want to sob. If only he weren't being so nice.

"I know coloring is important to you. It's how you escape and find peace. Did you know National Coloring Book Day is coming up?"

She shook her head. She hadn't known that.

"Yep. There's going to be a coloring day at Rawhide Ranch. A party. There will be contests you can enter, games, bounce houses, and snacks. I bet you wouldn't like to miss that."

She sucked in a breath and shook her head again. She would not want to miss a coloring day. That would make her very sad.

Master Tiago sat next to Master Rhodes on the couch. He set a hand on her lower back. "Daddy and I already discussed it. We think you need an incentive to earn the privilege of attending Coloring Book Day."

Eloise jerked her gaze to his and gasped. She'd never be able to be good long enough to earn something like that. Not in a million bagillion years.

Master Rhodes nodded. "He's right. We set up a sticker chart. Every time you do something kind or thoughtful or polite, you get to put a sticker on the chart. If you get it all filled up by the day of the party, we'll take you."

"Your crayons are going to stay in timeout for now, though, sweet girl," Master Tiago announced.

She managed to paste on her pouty face.

Master Tiago chuckled. "You have no idea how cute you are when you pout, sweet girl. It isn't going to work on either of us."

Master Rhodes narrowed his gaze at her. "I'm going to

spank you now, babygirl. To remind you that we care. We see you. We won't let you misbehave without repercussions. And then you're going to stand in the corner in timeout because I bet you'll hate that far more than the spanking."

She hmphed. "Nanny J makes me stand in timeout sometimes. I don't like it."

"Then maybe you'll learn to behave, yeah?" Master Rhodes lifted a brow as he ushered her to one side of his lap and then leaned her over his thighs.

It was Master Tiago who'd spanked her this morning. Her bottom still stung from that. She was a pretty naughty girl most days, but she didn't usually end up with a spanking more than once. This was going to hurt.

As Master Rhodes cuffed her wrists in one of his hands at the small of her back, Master Tiago slid his hands up her thighs and pulled her leggings and panties down to her knees.

She sucked in a breath and held it when they both touched her bare bottom. Her cheeks flushed. Something was different. The butterflies started flapping wildly in her tummy.

She squirmed. Wetness leaked between her legs. This wasn't supposed to happen. It hadn't ever happened before today. Why now?

She knew the answer. She was attracted to these two men. Physically. Having her bottom exposed to them was nothing like Nanny J or Master Derek.

When Master Tiago pushed her knees apart, she gasped. A whimper escaped. The butterflies seemed to take off, flapping harder as if they could escape.

"Are you okay, sweet girl?" Master Tiago asked.

She shook her head. She wasn't okay. Not even close.

"Your bottom is still pink from this morning," Master Rhodes pointed out, rubbing it with his hand, making her more and more aware of the sensation taking over her body. Arousal. Deep need.

She hadn't experienced arousal like this before today and never in the presence of another person. She was so embarrassed. She knew other Little girls talked about getting aroused from a spanking, but she'd never understood what they were referring to. Now she did. Just like this morning, for the second time today she was aroused from having her bottom exposed.

Would Master Rhodes and Master Tiago find out?

"Part your legs, sweet girl," Master Tiago ordered.

She hadn't realized she'd yanked them back together. She was squeezing her thighs tight to hide her confusing need. It didn't make sense. Why was she reacting so differently to being exposed to these two men than anyone else?

"Eloise..." Master Rhodes warned.

She pursed her lips and forced her knees apart, but she was trembling.

Suddenly, Master Tiago pulled her leggings and panties farther down her legs. He held them wider and put a pillow between her knees.

She moaned, the sound shocking her as it filled the room. "Please... You can't spank me right now, Daddy." The Daddy slipped out in her most vulnerable state. She was so aroused that she feared she would drip down her thigh and onto his jeans. Her knees were shaking badly and the pillow between them heightened every sense. No matter how hard she tried to squeeze her legs together, it felt like she was spread wide open, exposed, wet, so very, very needy.

"Why can't Daddy spank you, little one?" he asked in a gentle voice, his hand wandering all over her naked bottom and the backs of her thighs, making it impossible to think.

"You just can't. My... I... Uh..."

"I can smell your arousal, sweet girl," Master Tiago murmured. "Is that what's making you so nervous?"

She stiffened and held her breath. How mortifying. How could he know? Smell her? *Oh god.*

She squirmed, needing to get free so she could run and hide. She needed to get this weird feeling under control. If only these two men weren't so attractive.

"I don't... I can't... I've never..." Nothing that came out of her mouth made sense.

Daddy kept rubbing her heated skin. She was sure he'd spoken the truth about it still being pink. It stung a bit from this morning. If he swatted her, she would... She didn't know what would happen, but there was all this pressure building up that felt like it was going to explode out of her somehow.

"Daddy..." she begged.

He molded his palm to her butt cheek. "There's nothing wrong with being aroused while anticipating a spanking, babygirl. It happens to lots of Littles."

She shook her head. "Not me," she muttered.

Daddy drew in a deep breath. "That pleases us tremendously, little one. I hope that means you feel differently about us than anyone else."

She felt differently all right. Like she was going to lose her mind. She whimpered again. If only she could get free. If only... they would touch her... down there. The pressure. The need. It was unlike anything she'd ever felt. It was more intense tonight than it had been this morning.

Eloise had experienced arousal before, but not often and not like this. She'd never had an orgasm. She'd never been alone long enough to explore. Certainly not in any foster home or later in a girls' home or crowded shelter. And even here at Rawhide Ranch she had roommates. She would never risk touching herself.

"Take a breath, babygirl," Daddy said.

Daddy. The man holding her over his lap. Daddy? She wished that could be true forever and ever. It couldn't, but it felt so good. She wanted this to be real. She wanted him to hold her tight, spank her hard, and then touch her special parts. Her chest was pounding from that need.

Daddy's hand slid down until his fingers teased the fold between her thighs and her butt cheeks. He ran the tips along that crease, making her arch her chest off his lap. *Oh god*.

"We haven't discussed sex yet, babygirl. I don't know how you feel about having us touch you intimately. It seems awfully soon to ask you if you're interested in us that way. But we need to know a few things, honey. Please answer me honestly."

Her head was spinning. It was going to pop off her shoulders and roll across the floor. She dreaded his questions.

"How many men have you had sex with, Eloise?" Daddy asked.

She held her breath, not moving. Her cheeks were so hot they might catch on fire.

Daddy stopped stroking her skin, his hand gripping her bottom.

Papa's hand was on her thigh now, stroking between her legs, his fingers easing up toward her special place. "Tell us, Eloise. No one is going to judge you. We just need to know so we make the best choices."

Her lip was trembling as she admitted the truth. "None," she whispered.

There was a moment when neither man moved, a fleeting second, and then Daddy drew in a very long breath. "Okay. That's important. I'm glad I asked. Has anyone touched you, babygirl? Touched your pussy?"

She shuddered and shook her head. She was twenty-four years old, and she hadn't been with a man. How humiliating. She'd never even dated. Who would she date? She'd been in a homeless shelter for heaven's sake. She was lucky when she had clean clothes and a shower before she came here.

Papa was breathing heavily. She wanted to know what he was thinking. Did he think she was a freak? Probably.

"Did you get aroused when Papa spanked you this morning, babygirl?" Daddy asked gently.

She swallowed hard. She didn't want them to know. Her lip was trembling.

"It's okay, little one." Daddy started stroking her skin again, bringing the butterflies back into flight. "There's no reason to be embarrassed. I'm still going to spank you, but I need to know if you want Daddy to touch your pussy afterward and make you feel good."

Despite the pillow, she attempted to squeeze her knees as tight as possible, the exposure and intimacy overwhelming her. She wanted him to touch her down there more than she wanted her next breath. "Yes, Sir," she whispered.

"Okay, babygirl. Take a breath for me. I'm going to pepper your little bottom and then I'll make it feel better."

She couldn't obey that last order. She didn't remember how to breathe. There was no way. It didn't matter because Daddy swatted her bottom a moment later, making her gasp and draw in oxygen. The swat went straight to her private parts, lighting her on fire in a way she'd never imagined possible.

He spanked her other cheek next and then increased the pressure, setting up a rhythm, switching back and forth. When he lowered his hand to her upper thighs, she arched her chest off his lap. Her breasts felt tight and heavy. She

A CHEERFUL LITTLE COLORING DAY

didn't have big boobs. They were rather small with tiny nipples. The only reason she wore a bra was to cover the tight points. She didn't really need one. But right now, they felt huge.

She held her breath as Daddy continued to spank her, not releasing it until he stopped. She was a panting mess of nerves, sweating and needy and squirming. Her pigtails had loosened, and some locks of hair were stuck to her cheeks and forehead.

She was trembling, the need she felt had increased substantially while he spanked her. It was a total rush. Her bottom was on fire and her special parts wanted attention.

Daddy stroked her heated skin. Papa's hands were on her thighs.

"Please, Daddy... Papa... Please touch me."

Papa smoothed his hands up her inner thighs and held them wider, if that was possible. It felt obscene.

Daddy slid his hand down between her legs. The moment he touched her folds, she moaned. But that was nothing because the next thing he did was part her lower lips and stroke his fingers through her immense wetness.

"Oh god," she murmured. What was happening to her? The butterflies had grown in size. Maybe they were birds.

Daddy eased his fingers up higher until he touched the strange bundle of nerves that rested above her folds. Her clit. She knew what it was, but she'd never realized how unbelievably sensitive it could be.

"Daddy!" she cried out.

Daddy circled that tight bud, tapped it a few times, and then gave it a slight pinch.

Eloise exploded. She screamed at the same time. The birds flew out of her. Her entire body convulsed with the release.

Daddy eventually released the tiny nub, but he continued to circle it until she winced. It got too sensitive.

She turned to liquid, collapsing down over his thighs with her eyes closed. She was pretty sure her body was going to ooze between his legs and become goo on the floor.

Breathing heavily, she was only marginally aware of Daddy releasing her hands while Papa continued to stroke her thighs. In a moment, Daddy gently turned her over and cradled her against his chest.

Her leggings were still down around her ankles. Her soaking wet sex was exposed, but he pulled her dress over it, thankfully.

Kisses landed all over her face. "Thank you, babygirl. Thank you for trusting us to take care of you. Thank you for sharing that very intimate moment with us. Thank you for taking a chance on us and moving into our home." His words were reverent and sweet.

She curled into him, shivering in the aftermath of her orgasm. Every inch of her skin was tingling. Nothing she'd ever experienced had felt that good. A new longing creeped in. Something was missing. She knew what it was too. She wanted him to fill her pussy.

She finally tipped her head back. "Are you going to have sex with me now, Daddy?"

He smiled at her and kissed her forehead yet again. "No, babygirl. You're not ready for that."

She glanced at Papa who had inched closer and was cradling her with one arm behind her back. "You are so beautiful, sweet girl. The most precious, delightful Little girl ever."

She frowned at him. "I'm naughty."

He chuckled. "Naughty isn't necessarily a bad thing. As long as you do it in moderation and it doesn't consume your

A CHEERFUL LITTLE COLORING DAY

life. Naughty can be fun." He winked. "As you just found out."

Her eyes widened in surprise. "But I'm naughty all the time."

He shrugged. "I bet you'll find times to hold your naughty side at bay so you can fill that sticker chart." He lifted a questioning brow.

She pushed out her bottom lip. "I'll never be good enough to get those stickers."

"Sure you will," Papa disagreed. "You don't get negative points for being naughty. You won't be penalized for bad behavior. You simply earn the stickers when you make better choices."

She sniffled. That didn't sound quite as bad. Maybe she could do that. "Okay."

Both men chuckled as they hugged her tight in a group hug.

CHAPTER EIGHT

It felt strange when her Daddies left her alone in the bathroom later that night to take a bath and get ready for bed. She had thought they might insist on washing her themselves, and she was secretly a little disappointed, though she would never admit that.

"You're very quiet," Daddy said as he tucked her into bed in the cute pink nightie he'd presented her with before she went into the bathroom.

She shrugged as she snuggled in with Peaches. The bed was so very soft. She wanted to sleep here all night. Would she wake up later, feel unworthy, and move to the floor?

"Is the bed comfortable, sweet girl?" Papa asked her again, his expression filled with concern.

"It's the best bed ever, Sir."

"Are you going to stay in it, babygirl?" Daddy asked.

She shrugged again. "It's too...comfortable."

He chuckled. "We want you to stay in your bed. All night. If you can do that, you'll get a sticker in the morning." He leaned over to kiss her forehead before standing.

Next, he bent down and pulled something out from under the bed.

The railing. He lifted it up and snapped it into place. Patting the top of it, he said, "No getting out of bed. Understood?"

"Yes, Sir."

"You just went potty, and we didn't let you drink anything after dinner, so you shouldn't need to go to the bathroom, but if it makes you more comfortable, I can put a diaper on you."

She hesitated and then slowly shook her head. It wasn't because she didn't want him to diaper her. She did. But she wasn't ready for that kind of intimacy yet again today. Just the thought of these two Daddies parting her legs and wrapping her in a diaper made her squirm. They would be far more intimately involved in her care if she took that step. Much more than even the orgasm they'd given her earlier. At least she'd been on her tummy at the time.

Nanny J changed her diapers. Sometimes Miss Phoebe or another nursery attendant did too. But it wasn't the same. She had that same weird confusing feeling like she'd had with the spanking. Something about having these Daddies care for her made the butterflies return when that had never happened with anyone else.

"I hooked up the monitor, sweet girl," Papa said as he leaned over to kiss her cheek. He pointed to it in the corner of the room. "See the flashing red light in the top corner?"

She nodded.

"That means it's activated. We can see you from our cell phones during the night. If you need anything, just call out and it will alert us."

"Yes, Sir." She was struggling not to squirm. Everything

A CHEERFUL LITTLE COLORING DAY

they said and did seemed to make her belly flip around. What was wrong with her?

After another round of kisses to her face from both men, they eased from the room, leaving the door ajar. There was a night-light in the hallway that illuminated the room just enough to keep her from getting scared or confused.

She rolled onto her side, hugging Peaches close to her chest. Daddy would be going to work soon. Papa would be with her in the night. Most days, when she woke up, Daddy would be back and Papa would be gone.

It warmed her heart to know one of them would always be there with her. She knew a lot of the Littles with Daddies spent the day in the Littles' wing while their caregivers worked. Would she go to the Littles' wing at all since one of them was always home?

She kind of hoped not. She hadn't made friends there. In fact, she'd probably made enemies. The girls she'd been rooming with were undoubtedly relieved by her absence.

That made her feel sad. She didn't have friends, and it was all her fault. Rarely did she stop to consider that fact. She was always too busy maintaining her status as a disagreeable brat.

Could she be good? Papa said she was good. He said there was a very sweet girl inside. She just needed to let that Little girl out and hold on to her. Maybe he was right.

She certainly didn't want to miss out on the Coloring Book Day celebration. That was for sure. So she'd need to be good often enough to fill the sticker chart they'd attached to the fridge.

So far tonight, she'd earned two stickers. One for being polite and finishing her dinner. The other for taking her bath and getting ready for bed without complaint. It wasn't hard to earn the stickers.

Plus, she was relieved to learn she wouldn't be penalized for naughty behavior. No one would take the stickers away. But she might cause a delay in earning more of them if she spent too much time standing in the corner or getting her bottom spanked.

She curled into herself deeper at the memory of lying over Daddy's lap while he swatted her bottom. It still burned. She'd been spanked hard twice today. But more importantly, he'd touched her secret place and made her come. The experience would be imbedded in her mind for the rest of her life.

When would one of them do that again? Did she want them to? It had been embarrassing. She'd felt raw and exposed. Had they wanted to have sex with her? She couldn't be sure, but she thought they had. They said it was too soon. What did that mean? When would it be not too soon?

Wait. What was she even thinking? Sex. With whom? Both of them? She'd lost her mind. She'd never had sex with one man. She couldn't have sex with two men. And she had no experience with sex. She'd even told them as much. They wouldn't want to have sex with her.

She reached out a hand and touched the railing Daddy had lifted on the side of her bed. It comforted her in a weird way. It made her feel confined. Snuggly. Like a crib. She knew some Littles slept in an adult-sized crib. She'd never done that.

She would stay in her bed tonight. Because her Daddies wanted her to. They'd insisted. Even though it felt too nice for someone as naughty as her.

Papa said you were a good girl. Had he been telling her the truth or was he simply being nice? Of course he was being nice. Everyone knew she was naughty.

Maybe she could be naughty and good at the same time.

A CHEERFUL LITTLE COLORING DAY

When she was good, she got stickers. When she was naughty, she got spanked.

She shivered at the memory. Daddy had told her she would not always be granted an orgasm after a spanking. He'd made her look him in the eye and explained that she should not expect the two to go hand in hand. He'd even chuckled and said Little girls would get their bottoms spanked ten times a day if they thought they would always be permitted to come afterward.

She'd flushed deeply as he'd told her.

After that, her Daddies had made her stand in time out for five minutes and then given her a long list of rules.

No running in the house.

No climbing onto chairs to get to things that were up high.

No coloring on anything but paper.

No throwing her toys.

No going into either Daddy's or Papa's rooms without permission.

No climbing out of bed.

No television without permission.

No tantrums.

And no arguing with any rules. What Daddy and Papa said was law.

Following the list of rules, they had sat her down at the island, strapped her into her highchair again, and brought up a subject that made her uncomfortable.

School.

She'd explained that she hadn't finished high school and hadn't tried to get her GED. They'd told her what she'd already heard a dozen times from Master Derek—that she could get her GED right at Rawhide Ranch without ever leaving. There was an educational program at the Ranch where she could get her degree.

Why did they care? She didn't need some stupid high school diploma. It wouldn't do anything for her.

But Daddy and Papa had pushed, asking her a bunch of questions, telling her she would feel more empowered if she had her GED. It would open up a world of options for her.

She knew all that, but she wasn't interested.

Finally, they'd forced her to admit the truth. She was too embarrassed for anyone to test her and find out how far behind she was. It wasn't like she could just take some test. She hadn't ever done well in school, and she'd dropped out at the first opportunity.

Daddy had taken one hand. Papa had taken the other. They'd looked her in the eyes and told her she was bright and smart and perfectly capable. They'd assured her no one would judge her. It wasn't anyone's business what the testing showed. She would start from there, learn what she needed, and then take the test.

She wasn't at all sure she liked their plan, but they'd seemed to think it was important, and she didn't want to let them down, so she'd agreed to go take the test at least. She hadn't committed to doing anything after the test, but it couldn't hurt to at least find out what level she was at.

She wasn't stupid. She frowned again even now as she thought about it. She knew she wasn't dumb. She simply hadn't had any parents who cared how she did in school. No one had ever encouraged her or asked her questions. She'd moved from school to school often enough that she'd fallen further and further behind with each move until finally it had seemed futile. There'd been no way she could graduate. So, she'd given up and dropped out. Everyone

A CHEERFUL LITTLE COLORING DAY

thought she was a failure anyway. Why bother to prove them wrong?

Now she was nervous though. Why had she agreed to the assessment test anyway?

She flopped onto her back and stared at the ceiling. What if she took the test and her Daddies decided she wasn't worth keeping? She knew they would want to see the results. No way would they let her keep them to herself.

And then what? They would start pushing her to study. Studying wasn't fun. It wouldn't help her get a job washing dishes or making pancakes. It wouldn't help her get a job planting flowers or cleaning toilets. Those were the only jobs she was qualified to do.

A piece of her clenched inside though. Maybe they were right. Maybe she could be more, do more, have more in life if she applied herself. Nevertheless, she didn't like to hope for things like that. Hope always ended in disappointment. That included hoping these two Daddies would even keep her in the long run.

They were committed to helping her. They'd also told her many times today that they cared about her and had no interest in ever letting her go. But they hadn't spent day after day dealing with her tantrums and naughty behavior yet. One day—a day that landed her over their laps twice—didn't give them enough of a taste of Eloise Grace to make that kind of call.

It took a long time for her mind to calm down enough to fall asleep, but she finally did. And she slept all night in the comfy bed.

CHAPTER NINE

Eloise was very nervous when they arrived at the Ranch the next morning. Her Daddies had made an appointment first thing with Headmaster Jenkins.

Needless to say, she'd misbehaved several times between getting out of bed and leaving the house. She was squirming in her seat in the back of the car the entire drive, her bottom sore from the hard spanking she'd gotten when she refused to put her shoes on.

Luckily, her Daddies had kept their word about the sticker chart. She'd earned a sticker for staying in bed all night and another one for brushing her teeth without complaint.

She'd learned that earning the stickers didn't take much effort. Earning a sore bottom took a lot of effort. Being naughty was exhausting and drained her of energy.

Now, she was pouting, arms crossed, gaze toward the ground, feet shuffling along at a snail's pace as she followed her Daddies toward the large building located behind the Littles' wing.

Eventually, Papa got tired of waiting for her to pick up

the pace. He'd picked her up off the ground and carried her stiff body with one arm under her sore bottom.

Headmaster Jenkins greeted them when they reached the college and they were ushered into a conference room that contained nothing but a large table and chairs. At one end was a stack of paper and several pencils.

Papa carried her to the chair in front of the paper and pencils and settled her on a booster seat. When he pushed her to the table, she was grateful for the added height.

Headmaster Jenkins smiled warmly at her. He was very nice. He never once mentioned a single word of judgment about her lack of education. He simply asked her several questions to determine which level of testing to give her and then left for a few minutes to gather the appropriate testing material.

Daddy tipped her chin up and looked in her eyes. "This isn't a test for a grade, babygirl. I don't want you to worry about it. The results are only used to figure out what holes you have in your education so we can help prepare you for the GED. Do you understand?"

She nodded. She sort of understood. "You're going to be disappointed," she muttered.

Daddy pulled out the chair next to her so he was at eye level and met her gaze, holding her hand. "Never. No matter how you do on this test, it changes nothing. We don't care about your level of education, babygirl."

She looked away. "What if I'm stupid?"

He reached for her chin to drag her eyes back his direction. "You're not stupid, Eloise. I promise. You can't help what you haven't been taught. You're bright and perfectly capable. You didn't have a loving family who had your back and cheered you on. Now you do."

She flinched and glanced back and forth between Daddy and Papa. He didn't mean that. He couldn't.

A CHEERFUL LITTLE COLORING DAY

Papa squatted down next to Daddy and set a hand on her thigh. "All you can do is your best. It won't be any use if you refuse to try and waste the headmaster's time. We want you to answer all the questions you can. If you don't know the answer, you skip that one and move on."

"Okay," she mumbled.

"Good girl." Papa rose, kissed the top of her head, and scooted her to the table just as Headmaster Jenkins returned.

"Shall we get started?" The teacher beamed. "Your Daddies can go run errands and come back." He turned toward them. "It will take a few hours."

Eloise's chest tightened as the two men who'd taken her in twenty-four hours ago left her alone with the man. She didn't want them to leave. It made her sad. She was already attached to them.

That realization made her very nervous. She couldn't get attached to them. What a horrible idea. That was why she hadn't wanted to do this experiment in the first place. If she got too comfortable, she would be devastated when they decided they didn't want her anymore.

She was left alone to start the testing, and she stared at the paper for a few minutes before taking a deep breath and deciding to give this her best effort. There was no reason to bomb it on purpose. What good would that do? It wasn't like it was for a grade. She couldn't get kicked out of school or anything. She might as well take this risk and find out how far behind she was.

Three hours later, Eloise was a ball of nerves. She was shaking as the headmaster collected the test. He walked her back to the lobby where her Daddies were waiting.

She was so relieved to see them that she didn't stop herself from running to them and jumping into their arms.

"We're so proud of you, babygirl," Daddy said as he lowered onto one of the chairs and propped her in his lap.

She frowned. "How can you be proud of me? We don't even know how I did yet."

Papa patted her back. "Doesn't matter how you did. That's not the important part. What matters is that you took a chance and tried something that made you nervous. We don't care what the results are, sweet girl. We only care that you did your best and now we'll know what holes you have in your education."

"It was really hard," she told them. "I had to skip a lot of questions. And some I had to guess on."

"That's okay."

Headmaster Jenkins patted her shoulder. "Give me five minutes to run this through the scanner. I'll be right back."

"What?" Eloise stiffened as he walked away. "He's going to give us the results now? I thought it would be like next week or something."

Daddy patted her thigh. "Nope. Right now. You won't have to spend a single hour fretting. Headmaster Jenkins will tell us exactly what you need to do for your GED this morning."

She looked down at her lap, wringing her fingers together. "I don't know if I want to do that part, Daddy. You said all I had to do was take the test. You said I don't have to get my GED if I don't want to."

He hugged her close. "You don't have to do anything you don't want to do, babygirl. I meant every word. But we want you to consider it because we want you to be the best Little girl you can be."

She took a deep breath and let it out slowly. It would surely take years to finish her diploma. Forever and ever. And it would be boring and suck. She'd have to study and read and do math and stuff.

A CHEERFUL LITTLE COLORING DAY

Daddy was still holding her, and she leaned her head on his shoulder, trying not to think about the test results. She wasn't sure why she was so nervous. Like they'd told her many times, it wasn't a test of her intelligence. It was a test of her knowledge. She couldn't help what she hadn't been exposed to.

Daddy rubbed her back, helping calm her while she took deep breaths, inhaling his scent. She really liked when one of them held her like this. It made her heart rate slow down. She felt loved and protected, which wasn't something she'd experienced often in this life.

She jumped on his lap when the door opened and Headmaster Jenkins stepped back into the room. He held up a packet of paper and nodded over his shoulder. "Come on back to the conference room and I'll go over the results with you."

Eloise was trembling. She held on to her Daddy's neck so tight that he didn't even try to set her down. He carried her into the conference room with her legs wrapped around his waist.

When they stepped inside, Papa pulled out a chair, sat, and reached for her.

She let Daddy pass her off to Papa, who immediately pulled her in close, held her tight, and kissed her temple. "Take a breath, sweet girl."

Daddy sat next to them.

Headmaster Jenkins smiled as he sat across from them. "No reason to fret, little one. You're not nearly as behind as you seemed to fear." He slid a stack of papers toward them.

Eloise didn't look. She turned her face toward Papa's neck and wrapped her arms tight around him.

Headmaster Jenkins tapped the papers. "In most areas, you're at a high school level. Even though you might not have done well in high school or finished, you still picked up information just by living. Your reading comprehension could use some work, but if you spend time reading every day, you'd be able to retake this test and do much better in no time."

She sniffled. "Really?"

He nodded when she glanced at him.

"But I don't like reading," she pointed out.

"I bet you would if you were reading something that interested you. A lot of people think they don't like reading because they've only read what was required for classes and didn't care for the subject matter. Why don't you take a few books home from the library and figure out what interests you?"

"That's a great idea," Daddy agreed.

"If you want to get your GED, we have classes that meet here every day. Whatever fits your schedule. A lot of Littles like to come for four hours in the morning and then do the rest of their studies at home in the afternoon and evening," the professor explained.

"That's a lot of studying," she pointed out.

"You can work at whatever pace you want. The more time you spend dedicated to learning, the quicker you'll be able to pass your GED exam," he reminded her.

"I don't know..." It sounded like a lot of work to her and for what? She wasn't smart. She wasn't going to become a lawyer or a doctor or anything.

Papa rubbed her back. "How about if we check out a few books so you can read them at home, and we can discuss this over the next few days, okay?"

She nodded noncommittally.

The headmaster stood. "You can go through the test results in more detail and see where her weaknesses are. Every student here is different. We create an individualized

A CHEERFUL LITTLE COLORING DAY

lesson plan with suggestions that will help each pupil meet their goals in whatever timeframe they choose."

"Thank you so much." Daddy stood and shook the teacher's hand.

Headmaster Jenkins smiled broadly at Eloise as Papa also stood with her in his arms. "If you're interested, we offer a variety of college options here too."

She gasped, her eyes going wide. "I'm not smart enough for college."

Papa stiffened, his hand stilling on her back. "That's bologna, malony, Eloise. You're as bright as anyone I know. If you want to go to college, we'll make it happen. Don't ever let me hear you say you're not smart again, or I'll take you over my knee and spank you so hard you won't be able to sit for a week."

Her face heated as she met his gaze. He was serious. Surely, he was wrong. She'd never been smart. And she couldn't believe he was talking about sending her to college when she'd just moved in with them yesterday. He couldn't be serious.

She glanced at Daddy. He nodded. "He's right, babygirl. You can do anything you set your mind to. We'll make sure of it."

She licked her lips. "I could never go to college. I don't have any money and I need to work to pay for my room and board."

Headmaster Jenkins slipped from the room while she was making her case.

Daddy rounded to stand so that no space existed between them, making Eloise a Daddy sandwich filling. She was the peanut butter. They were the bread. Maybe with the crusts on, though, considering how sternly they were both looking at her.

Daddy cupped her face. "I know you've only been with us a day, babygirl, but we've both known we cared about you long before yesterday. We don't want your stay with us to be temporary. We've never thought about it in those terms. We want our home to be your home. We want you to decorate your room however you'd like. We never want you to worry about food or clothes or where you might sleep at night. That includes money. Rawhide Ranch has a beneficiary program that covers educational plans, but no matter what, Papa and I intend to take care of everything you need."

She glanced back and forth between them, not letting herself believe him. It was too scary. Too risky. Already she knew her heart was going to break when things went south. Every moment she let herself believe she could have a future with them burrowed her deeper into the sorrow that would follow when it ended.

Papa shifted her weight in his arms. "We know you enjoyed working with Chef Connor, and if you decide you'd like to continue that, we'll make that happen, but it's not mandatory. We would rather see you pursuing your dreams. You don't need to worry about where your next meal will come from ever again, sweet girl. It will come from our kitchen. All your meals."

"That's right," Daddy agreed. "If you'd like to spend every day working on your studies so you can get your GED and maybe even start taking college classes, we'll support you, emotionally, physically, and financially."

Tears slid down her cheeks. Her lip trembled. "You can't mean that," she whispered.

"We do," Papa insisted. "We mean every word. And we'll show you every day until you believe us."

"Let's go home," Daddy added. "We can discuss this more later. You're exhausted."

Eloise said nothing as they left the Ranch's university

A CHEERFUL LITTLE COLORING DAY

building and headed for the car. She let Daddy buckle her into the back seat and stared out the window as they drove... home. Was their house really her home?

She shook the idea from her head. *Don't let yourself believe any of this.*

She closed her eyes. Maybe she was dreaming. Or maybe she was having a nightmare. She would certainly agree with the latter when everything went to shit.

By the time they got back to the house, Eloise was sullen. She could feel her naughty side coming to the surface. She tried to stop it, but she couldn't. She was itching to get out of this situation and fast. She had to go back to the dorm. If she stayed with these two Daddies, she would grow attached and end up sad for the rest of her life.

It would be better not to taste the fruit than to nibble at it and find out how good it could be only to have it taken away.

As Papa helped her out of the car, she glanced around. She could take off running, but where would she go? It wasn't like she could walk back to Rawhide Ranch. She might get hit by a car. Besides, did she really belong at Rawhide Ranch? A naughty girl like her who couldn't make friends and didn't want stupid friends anyway.

Daddy set a hand on her back and led her into the house. "How about a bottle and a nice nap?" he suggested.

She nodded, feeling kind of numb and detached. A bottle sounded nice, especially if he was going to hold her. What difference did it make now? She was already half in love with these Daddies. The damage was done. She might as well let them coddle her for a while longer. When she finally left, she wasn't likely to know this sort of kindness again for a long time if ever.

She was too emotionally exhausted to take off running.

She didn't even have a plan. She might as well accept their misguided kindness for a while longer.

When she realized he was waiting for an answer, she tipped her head back and met his gaze. "Okay, Daddy."

Both men seemed extraordinarily pleased at her acceptance. They ushered her inside and scurried around preparing her a bottle.

After glancing at each other, Papa nodded and took the bottle from Daddy. It felt like they'd exchanged a silent battle of wills, determining who got to feed her. Papa won. Was she really worth all that?

She felt more cared for than ever as Daddy took her hand and led her to the nursery.

Papa sat in the rocking chair and reached for her.

She climbed up into his lap and snuggled against his warm chest.

Papa smiled at her as he settled her in his arms, leaning her back before bringing the bottle to her lips.

She accepted it eagerly and was pleased to find that whatever was in the bottle tasted really yummy. Like a vanilla protein shake.

No one had ever fed her a bottle before. Nanny J had offered her bottles in the nursery a few times, but she'd declined. It hadn't seemed like fun if she had to hold it herself.

She stared into Papa's eyes as he smiled at her. Something loosened in her tummy as she suckled. Like a tight knot that refused to hold on even though she willed it to.

She couldn't seem to stay in the headspace she'd been in while they were driving. It was too hard to grasp on to that anger and sadness and maintain her resolve not to let herself get close to these two Daddies.

Not with Papa grinning with such pleasure and Daddy leaning in close, also looking like he'd won the lottery. Not with Papa holding her in his lap, stroking her hip while she sucked. Not with Daddy reaching out to brush a lock of hair from her forehead and then bending down to kiss her temple, lingering as if he couldn't stand to be parted from her.

Her bitterness dissolved to a simmering worry as she let Papa treat her the way she'd always prayed someone would. Twenty-four years was a long time to hope for someone to care about her, and suddenly she had two Daddies who seemed to sincerely want to love her.

If she was honest, no one had ever come this close to loving her before. It's not like she'd been treated to a full day of happiness only to have it taken away. The longest anyone had ever pretended to care had been an hour or so when she'd been dropped off at a new foster home. It never lasted, which had eroded her trust over the years.

This was different though. It had been much longer than an hour. What reason would her Daddies have to trick her and hurt her?

The only problem was they didn't know her well enough yet to be as sure as they acted. She could be very naughty. She would be sometimes. Even though they said there was nothing she could do that would make them turn her away, they were mistaken. Deep down she knew it.

But for now, she couldn't bring herself to rock this boat. She was too comfortable, too... happy. She kept sucking, her eyes growing heavy. The arms around her held her tight, keeping her safe, making her feel things she hadn't known were in the cards for her.

When the bottle was empty, Papa set it aside and slipped a different nipple in her mouth.

She suckled it for a moment before realizing nothing was coming out of it. Blinking, she looked up at him. He was still rocking her, staring at her face, holding the pacifier in her mouth. "You're safe, sweet girl," he murmured. "Everything is going to be okay."

She roused slightly more when Daddy lifted her out of Papa's arms. "Can I put a diaper on you so you don't have to worry about going potty during your nap, babygirl?"

She hesitated only a moment and then nodded. She was too tired to argue, and the diaper sounded so nice. It was the only thing missing from the scene. The nursery, the bottle, the pacifier... All fantasies she'd had over the years of being nurtured and loved. Adding a diaper would make everything exactly perfect.

Eloise tried not to think about the fact that she was fully exposed to her two Daddies as Daddy removed her leggings and panties while Papa lifted her dress up to her chest and held her hands out of the way.

Daddy was quick. He slid a diaper under her without hesitation. The only thing that caused her to become more alert was when he spread some kind of ointment on her folds.

He awakened that same feeling she'd had yesterday when he'd touched her intimately like that and made her orgasm. She squirmed and arched her chest as he touched that sensitive bundle of nerves, moaning behind the pacifier.

A few seconds later, he pulled the front of the diaper between her legs and fastened it at her waist.

Papa leaned over to kiss her forehead. "Shhh. Let us take care of you, sweet girl."

She realized he was soothing her because she was still wiggling and whimpering. Her secret parts were awake now and needy, but no one acknowledged that fact.

Papa scooped her up, carried her to her bed, and lowered her to the mattress. "Do you want me to take your dress off while you nap, sweet girl?"

A CHEERFUL LITTLE COLORING DAY

She found herself nodding, though she couldn't imagine why.

Papa wasted no time lifting her dress over her head, baring her breasts to his gaze. He didn't stare at her though. He immediately pulled the covers up to her chin and tucked Peaches in with her.

Both Daddies kissed her cheeks again and smiled down at her before lifting the side railing up and locking it into place.

"If you need us, just call out, okay?" Daddy said.

She nodded behind the pacifier.

They lingered a few more moments before leaving her. If she wasn't mistaken, they would have rather stayed and watched her sleep.

Eloise turned her head as they left the room. Her chest tightened. She wanted them to stay. She liked it when they were with her. She wouldn't ask for something so silly, but she felt their loss immediately.

This was so real, especially now that she was in her bed, naked except for the diaper. She'd never felt so... right. She snuggled Peaches against her bare chest and nuzzled his fur against her nose.

The pacifier felt good in her mouth. It was better than her thumb. The contents of the bottle had filled her just right so her tummy wasn't grumbling. The diaper made her relax at a level she only ever managed while wearing one. She knew she would end up using it and Daddy and Papa wouldn't care.

Was this okay? She feared she was falling too hard for them. She already felt like she was at home in this house. She couldn't wait to wake up and see them smiling at her. How long could she stay in this bubble before it burst?

Maybe, just maybe, she was finally where she was meant

to be, and no one would turn her away and make her feel unwanted and unloved.

She wouldn't let herself fully believe that yet, but she didn't have the strength to run from them. She wanted this so badly.

She wanted to belong to them.

She let out a deep breath and slid into the best sleep of her life.

CHAPTER TEN

When Eloise woke up from her nap, Papa was there immediately. After he lowered the railing for her bed, he kissed all over her face, making her giggle. She was glad because it made the next several minutes less awkward.

He lifted her from the bed, carried her to the changing table, and cleaned her up without saying anything or making a fuss about it.

Eloise held her breath. She was naked. It should have been awkward, but he didn't let it be. The strap he'd used to secure her waist to the table made her insides flip around, and she couldn't stop herself from lifting her hands to cover her breasts.

Her nipples were hard points. If he noticed she was wet between her legs, he didn't say anything. As soon as he discarded her diaper and the wipes, he met her gaze. "Another diaper or panties, sweet girl?"

"Panties, Papa," she murmured. It was one thing to nap in a diaper. She wasn't ready to waddle around their home in one.

Papa unfastened the strap and lifted her off the table, setting her naked body on her feet before helping her into a pair of panties, her leggings, and lastly, her dress. He smiled when he was finished. "There." He lifted her off the floor by the waist so she was flattened against his chest eye to eye. "Thank you for letting me take care of you, sweet girl. I know that was hard. It means the world to me."

She cupped his face and smiled at him. "Thank you, Papa."

He lowered her to her feet and took her hand. "How about some lunch?"

"Where's Daddy?"

"Sleeping." He put a finger to his lips as they stepped into the hall and didn't speak again until they were in the kitchen. "He has to work tonight. He'll sleep until I leave for work and then spend the evening with you."

She frowned. "That's not enough sleep."

"Yeah. Normally, he'll sleep most of the morning, but today he wanted to be with you for the assessment testing."

"Oh." The funny butterflies in her tummy returned, flipping around at the thought of Master Rhodes forgoing sleep to be with her for something as important as this morning. She'd never had anyone do something that kind for her.

She was quiet as Papa lifted her into the highchair, fastened her, and locked the tray into place. The next thing he did was bring her sticker chart over and the row of colorful star stickers.

"We were so proud of you for being brave this morning and for taking a risk and letting us care for you before your nap. I know both of those things took courage. You didn't complain once. You deserve five stickers. Would you like to put them on the chart?"

A CHEERFUL LITTLE COLORING DAY

She grinned as he peeled them off one at a time and handed them to her. She felt an odd sense of pride. She'd been good. She'd gotten rewarded. Papa and Daddy were happy.

What would happen when she misbehaved though? Would they be mad and grow tired of her antics? Maybe she could be good. It was a lot more fun. It was also scary because it set her up for hurt.

People weren't kind to her for long. They always inevitably disappointed her. As she watched Papa hang her sticker chart on the fridge and fill a sippy cup with apple juice, she struggled to imagine him disappointing her, but that didn't help her shake the fear.

"What would you like for lunch, sweet girl?" he asked as he handed her the drink.

"Peanut butter," she declared, giggling.

"Again?"

She nodded. "I like peanut butter. It's my favorite."

"Did you eat a lot of it as a child?"

She hesitated, biting her lip. She hadn't told them the specifics about her childhood. They hadn't asked yet.

Papa pulled out the white bread and peanut butter, but left them on the island to approach her. He sat on the stool next to her so they were eye to eye. His hand came to her cheek. "Tell me about peanut butter, Eloise," he encouraged gently.

She glanced down at her hands on the tray and fiddled her fingers together as the memories flitted through her mind. She could still see the face of her third foster mother, smirking at her. It made her tense.

Papa waited patiently, stroking her cheek with his thumb.

Finally, she drew in a breath. "I ate it often at my first

two homes. I loved it. Then at my third home, the case worker told the new foster mom it was my favorite food." Her breath hitched and she swallowed hard to fight the tears that wanted to fall.

Papa's hand stilled before he dropped it to the tray and clasped both of her hands in his larger one. He kept silent though.

Eloise blurted out the rest of the story in a rush of words. "She said I was too naughty for peanut butter, so she fed me bologna every day. It was gross. I hated it." She shuddered at the memory.

"Oh, sweetie..." Papa slid closer and wrapped his arms around her upper body. "I'm so sorry. That was inappropriate and nasty. No one should treat a child that way."

Eloise held her breath to keep from crying. She didn't want to let herself be sad. That was a long time ago. She wasn't there anymore. That foster mom couldn't hurt her.

When Papa pulled back, he set his hands on her shoulders and looked her in the eye. "We will never ever, ever punish you by taking away food or making you eat something you don't like."

She nodded. There was a lump in her throat.

"How about after lunch, you make a list for us. Two lists. One of your favorite foods and one of the foods you hate."

She nodded, fighting tears again.

"From now on, you may eat peanut butter for lunch every day if you want. I can make it with grape jelly or strawberry jam or honey. Whatever you'd like. The peanut butter will never go away. We will encourage you to eat fruits and vegetables so you have a healthy balanced diet, but you can choose which ones you like and don't like." He lifted a brow. "Got it?"

She nodded again. Her voice was tentative when she

asked her next burning question. "Do you have marshmallow fluff?"

He chuckled. "Nope. But I'll buy some next time I'm at the store. Is that what you like with your peanut butter?"

She shrugged. "I don't know. I've never tried it. I once saw a girl at school who brought that every single day. I was jealous."

"Then we'll get some and you can try it."

"My foster mom said it would rot my teeth."

Papa chuckled. "I'm positive marshmallow fluff won't do any more damage than jelly would. We'll just brush your teeth after you eat so it doesn't stay stuck to them. How does that sound?"

Eloise stared at him, grinning wider than she thought she'd ever grinned before. Her heart was beating fast too. Papa seemed so sincere. He acted like he really cared. Both of her Daddies did. It was the nicest feeling in the world.

She shuddered with worry as he made her a sandwich with peanut butter and honey. She couldn't speak. Words were stuck in her throat. All she could do was nod to choose the honey over jelly and the orange over the apple.

She ate her favorite food in silence, watching her Papa closely as he ate his fancy sandwich filled with meat and cheese and condiments.

When she was all finished, she asked another question. "Do you have any bologna?"

He was putting everything away and he turned toward her. "No. I've never liked it. Daddy doesn't either."

She shivered. "Good. It's gross."

He chuckled as he released her tray and then the straps.

"I won't fall, you know. I'm not really a baby," she pointed out as he unfastened the three-point buckle with the nylon straps that came around her waist and between her legs.

He set his hands on the sides of her highchair and met her gaze. "Of course you won't fall. You won't fall out of bed either. Nor would you wet your panties if you slept in them. You could surely sleep without a stuffie too. I bet you could get an apartment in town, live alone, get a job, dress in adult clothes, walk across the street without getting hit by a car, cook your own meals, take showers instead of baths without any help."

He smiled at her and leaned in closer to kiss her nose. "But some people enjoy the submission of age play. They feel more like themselves when they let someone else take care of them. Some prefer to be older. Some younger. You're welcome to experiment with other ages if you want, Eloise. We would never hold you back from finding what makes you happy. But, based on everything we know about Eloise Grace, I suspect the one thing you're certain about is that you enjoy very young age play. There may be a lot of unanswered questions in your head about the future and what you might like to do with your life, but your place in the age-play community isn't one of them, is it, sweet girl?"

She stared at him for a long time, finally shaking her head. "How did you know?" she asked in awe.

He lifted her from the highchair and set her on her feet, taking her hand to lead her outside. As soon as he settled on the porch swing, he hauled her up with him. This time, he didn't settle her next to him. He angled her onto his lap before pushing gently with his feet so they started swinging.

He slid his hand to her hair, eased her head against his shoulder, and kissed the top of her head. "Since Daddy and I work in security, we keep a close eye on everything that happens at Rawhide Ranch. We told you we've been paying close attention to you for quite some time. We know you gravitate to the Nursery. Even when you're not there, you tend to slide into younger behavior."

Eloise thought about his words for a while, enjoying the sway of the swing and the beat of his heart against her.

After a while, he spoke again. "Eventually, we'll sit down and discuss your preferences, figure out how much of the time you like to be in a younger headspace and how much you'd prefer not to. We'll find out what works best for you and make it your new reality."

It was all too good to be true. None of this could be real. She was scared out of her mind that she was sleeping and would soon wake up and feel sadder than ever. She couldn't continue to be good like this. She felt her naughty side coming to the surface.

Papa gave her a squeeze and released her, grabbing her around the waist and setting her on her feet. He held her hips and looked her in the eye. "I can feel your tension. You were all nice and soft and relaxed and then you got tight and stiff." He narrowed his gaze.

She swallowed and looked down. He could read her mind.

"Look at me, Eloise." His voice was firm.

She took a breath and lifted her gaze, but she knew her face was scrunched up in defiance.

He was... smiling? Almost. Just the corners of his lips. "I know your instinct is to sabotage this arrangement. You can have a tantrum if you want, sweet girl. It won't change anything. You can have tantrums every day if you'd like. Ten of them. Twenty. You'll be exhausted and your bottom will be sore, and you'll get lonely from standing in the corner, but we won't let you down."

She gasped. How did he know?

He nodded. "We're in your corner now. We knew we wanted you to be our Little girl even before we approached you yesterday. We're even more certain of it today than ever. You can try to ruin it, but you will not succeed. Unless you prove to us that you truly don't care for us and you're not attracted to us, you're ours, Eloise. Forever."

She blinked at him, all of the wind going out of her sail. She wavered between turning and running away, dropping to the ground to have a tantrum, or throwing everything around her that wasn't nailed down. But he was holding her shoulders and looking her in the eye. He ruined her growing naughty urge.

His voice was soft and firm at the same time when he spoke again. "We don't care if you're naughty, Eloise. If that's what you need, go for it. We'll be firm and strict with you, because we know that's also what you need. To be seen. To be heard. You need someone to care enough not to walk away no matter what you do. You've found that in us."

Eloise gulped. This couldn't be possible.

"We will be here no matter what you decide. No matter who you want to be. We'll always be your cheerleaders, encouraging you to be the best you, but we won't force you to do anything you don't want. If you want to get your GED, we'll support you. If you want to go to college, we'll make that happen too. If you want to make perfectly round pancakes in the Ranch kitchen, we'll drive you there ourselves."

She gasped. "How did you know about the pancakes?"

He grinned. "We've been paying attention. Your fruit tarts are perfection too." He winked.

Her eyes popped out of her head. She licked her lips. "I like making pretty foods."

"The cake and tarts you made for Moira's baby shower were almost too pretty to eat. Your creations are both beautiful and delicious, sweet girl. You can be happy or sad. You can be well-behaved or naughty. You can be as Little as you want as often as you want. None of that will change how Daddy and I feel."

"How can you know that?" Her head was spinning.

"I told you, we've been paying attention." He slid one hand to the middle of her back and pulled her closer until their faces were inches apart. "I need to know one thing, Eloise."

Her breath hitched. She licked her lips as she inhaled his scent. He was so close to her. She was rattled, her body tingling. Feelings she'd only experienced two times before—after her spankings yesterday—arose again.

Papa's hand slid up higher between her shoulder blades, anchoring her in place, holding her captive. Or maybe his eyes did that. "Do you want me to kiss you?"

She stared at him and slowly nodded.

"On the lips, sweet girl. Do you want me to kiss you like a man?"

She nodded again, her face heating.

"Have you ever been kissed?"

She shook her head, her face heating further.

"I know you got aroused yesterday and had an orgasm when we touched you, but do you want a physical relationship with us?" His expression was so earnest.

She glanced at the door. Daddy was sleeping inside the house. "With both of you?" she whispered.

"Yes. I mean that's what Rhodes and I want. We'd like you to be our Little girl. We'd like to take care of every one of your needs." His voice deepened. "We'd also like to have you in our beds. Have you as a woman."

She sucked in a breath. Her entire body was on fire. That nub between her legs was pulsing with need, reminding her how Daddy had touched it yesterday. "At the same time? Both of you?" She needed more details. She needed to be sure she understood what Papa was asking for.

"Sometimes. Sometimes just me and you. Sometimes just Daddy and you. Sometimes all three of us. How does that make you feel?" His hand stilled on her back while he waited. He was anxious about her response.

Eloise had never made anyone anxious in her life. She'd never had anyone pay this close attention to her either. "It makes me feel special." Her bottom lip started quivering as emotions overwhelmed her. "It makes me feel scared."

Papa set his forehead against hers. "You are so very special. Tell me about the scared part. Are you worried about having sex?"

Her cheeks heated ten thousand degrees. She shrugged. "Maybe. Mostly I'm afraid you'll change your mind." Her lip quivered uncontrollably. "I'd be devastated," she admitted. It was hard for her. She wasn't usually this open. She'd never shared her feelings like this.

"I understand that, sweet girl. We both do. I'm making a promise to you that we will not change our minds. No matter what you do. I know your instinct is to pull out all the stops and misbehave every moment of the day to prove to yourself that you're not worth loving, but it won't work. I'm making that promise to you. We won't even get angry."

She looked down.

He tipped her chin back up. "I'm sure you've noticed that some Littles are brats. They like to misbehave all the time for a variety of reasons. Mostly they like to be punished. They enjoy having their bottoms spanked or being denied certain privileges."

"I don't think I'm like them, Sir."

He smiled. "I don't either, Eloise. I think you misbehave in order to keep people at arm's length. They can't hurt you if you never develop a relationship with them.

A CHEERFUL LITTLE COLORING DAY

When you misbehave in the nursery, it keeps other Littles from wanting to play with you. That way if you don't make friends, they can't leave you. When you're disobedient in front of caregivers, you keep them at arm's length so they can't give up on you and leave you too."

She gasped. *How did he know so much? He was a psychic Papa.*

For a long time, he continued to hold her gaze, his face so close to hers that her heart was racing and her panties grew damp. She was aroused. Partly because he was so sexy and so close, but also because she'd never felt so understood in her life.

"Are you still going to kiss me?" she whispered boldly.

"I'd love nothing more. Would you like me too?"

"Will Daddy be mad?" She kept worrying about leaving him out.

"Nope. I promise. He'd like to kiss you too, but we talked about it. We don't want to rush you. We'll kiss you when you're ready. Doesn't matter who goes first. Eventually, we'll both kiss you so often you won't remember who kisses you more." His smile slayed her.

"Do other Little girls have two Daddies?"

He winked. "Only the lucky ones."

She smiled. It felt natural. It felt good. "I think I'd like you to kiss me, Papa." She licked her lips again and lowered her gaze to his mouth. What would it feel like? She wanted to know.

Papa's hand slid to the back of her head. He cupped her there, stroking her neck with his long fingers. After a beat, he angled his head slightly to one side and closed the distance.

The moment his lips touched her, she leaned into him. Her knees were weak. It didn't seem like they would support her. She lost track of time and space as he gently nibbled her lips before increasing the pressure and guiding her closer.

She moaned against his mouth, loving the feeling. It was so intimate. She'd never felt this close to another human before. Not even yesterday over Daddy's lap. He'd given her an orgasm, but he hadn't kissed her. The kiss meant more than the fondling.

When Papa's tongue slid along the seam of her lips, she opened for him, tentatively tasting him while he did the same. He didn't plunge into her mouth. He kept the kiss sweet and slow. He let her get used to him. She appreciated it.

Suddenly a noise behind her made her jerk back and glance over her shoulder just as Daddy stepped onto the porch.

He cringed. "I'm so sorry. I didn't mean to interrupt."

Eloise's cheeks heated again, flamed. She felt very awkward. She'd been kissing Papa while Daddy slept. How much had he seen? Was he mad? Papa had told her he would not be, but he could have been wrong.

She dropped her gaze, shuddering as she tried to wrench free of Papa's embrace.

He didn't let her go though, and a moment later, Daddy was sitting next to him on the swing. Daddy reached out and slid a hand up Eloise's arm. "I'm very sorry, babygirl," he repeated. "I saw you through the sliding door and wanted to join. I should have waited."

Papa stroked her back. "Don't be embarrassed, sweet girl. We don't ever want you to hold back with us. Not when we're alone or together."

She glanced at Daddy. "You're not mad?"

He shook his head. "I'm so happy. You two must have had quite the conversation to precede that kiss."

"We did," Papa admitted. "I was telling Eloise that she

could be anyone she wanted to be, and it won't change how we feel. Including however naughty she likes to behave."

"Ah. He's right." Daddy clutched her biceps.

"Are you going to have sex with me *now?*" she asked timidly, her mind wrapping around that not unappealing idea. She desperately wanted to know what it would feel like, though she was scared to find out how all three of them might have sex together.

Papa shook his head. "No, sweet girl. We're a long way from having sex. We definitely got things out of order yesterday when Daddy gave you an orgasm before either of us kissed you, but there's a lot to cover between kissing and penetration."

She swallowed, having no idea what he was talking about. She wasn't dumb. She knew what sex entailed. It was when a man put his penis inside a woman. She'd heard plenty of women at the shelter talk about it when they didn't think she was listening. Some of them enjoyed it. A lot of them said it wasn't worth it and it was a chore.

She hadn't heard anyone at Rawhide Ranch refer to sex as a chore. In fact, most of the Littles she'd eavesdropped on when they discussed sex acted like they were going to swoon. Who was right?

Until yesterday she hadn't cared. Now, her curiosity was piqued. She also had a lot of questions, especially if she was going to have two Daddies.

Squirming as possibilities went through her mind, she glanced at Daddy's lips and licked her slightly swollen ones.

Papa released his hold on her and angled her toward Daddy who slid his palm from her arm to her back. "Would you like Daddy to kiss you too, babygirl?" he asked.

She nodded. Maybe this was strange. Two men sitting before her, both of them wanting to kiss her. But it felt right, and she certainly didn't do much of anything in her life by any conventional standards.

Daddy set his lips on hers, equally gently. However, he pulled her tighter a moment later, grasped her chin, and angled her head to one side. He deepened the kiss quicker, sliding his tongue into her mouth as if he were starving.

Goosebumps rose up her arms and down her legs. The butterflies went crazy inside her. She gripped her thighs together as that need she'd learned about yesterday took hold of her again.

He tasted like mint and Daddy. Like hope and sunshine. Like smiles and attagirls. He tasted like home.

When he released her, they were all three breathing heavily. Even Papa who hadn't been involved in that second kiss but was seemingly just as affected. His hand was on her lower back. His breaths were as unsteady and erratic as hers and Daddy's.

Papa leaned in and kissed her cheek. "You're precious, Eloise. Every inch of you. Do not ever forget it."

She flushed as they crowded her, holding her close, touching her everywhere. Their hands slid up and down her back, her butt, her thighs. They stroked her arms and neck and cheeks. They didn't touch her breasts or between her legs, but she was affected by them as if they had, and she wished they would.

No way would she say that out loud. How embarrassing, but she thought it.

Finally, Papa leaned back and looked at Daddy. "You're going to be exhausted. You didn't get enough rest."

He shrugged. "I couldn't sleep. All I could think about was this precious girl somewhere in our house. I kept picturing her playing or swinging or eating another popsicle." His voice deepened as he met her gaze. "I kept wondering if she was smiling at you or giggling."

Her face flamed. She didn't laugh often. She'd never had a reason to. Most of the time she felt angry. Ever since she'd come home with these two Daddies yesterday, she'd felt lighter and happier.

Please let this last.

CHAPTER ELEVEN

Rhodes turned off his alarm, rolled over in his bed, and smiled. He'd never been happier in his life. The sweetest Little girl was in his home. She was gradually relaxing. The stiffness in her shoulders eased more every hour. The frown lines between her eyes, earned from years of mistrust, began to dissipate.

He caught her smiling sometimes when she didn't know he was watching. She did so when she was coloring or drawing, which made him wonder what she thought about while she was doing art.

He didn't ask. She was entitled to her private thoughts. But he hoped they were about him and Tiago and her new lease on life.

It had been a week since she'd moved in with them. He prayed she wasn't still thinking of this arrangement as temporary. She'd blossomed in so many ways. She came to them eagerly without hesitation now. She sat on their laps. Kissed and hugged and relaxed into their embraces.

She seemed to easily transition between them when one of them was home and the other at work. The relationship they each had with her was slightly different. Tiago usually took her outside, pushed her on the swing or built sandcastles with her. Rhodes often rocked her and read to her.

His heart was huge today because they'd had a serious discussion with her about school last night and she'd agreed to take classes to work on her GED. They had a schedule worked out.

They would all eat breakfast together when Rhodes got home from work in the mornings. Rhodes would go to bed. Tiago would take her and pick her up from her classes afterward. Tiago would feed her lunch, spend quality time with her, and put her down for a nap before he left for work.

Rhodes would get up an hour later and wake her from her nap. He would oversee her afternoon studies, feed her dinner, and then spend time with her.

It was a win-win. He and Tiago had worked it all out. They were both pleased with the arrangement. He hoped Eloise was too.

It wouldn't be smooth and perfect of course. They couldn't schedule Eloise's tantrums. Those happened whenever the muse struck her, usually once a day, sometimes twice.

She was testing them. They would outlast her every time. Neither of them flinched. They let her throw her fits, spanked her or put her in time out, and then held her afterward and told her how special she was.

Rhodes had noticed her glancing at them sometimes when she was on the floor kicking or throwing something. It was difficult not to laugh. It was incredibly hard for her to trust them to stay by her side, and he understood that. It had taken twenty-four years for her to prove that no one would ever care enough about her to stick around. It would take a long time to prove to her

A CHEERFUL LITTLE COLORING DAY

that she was wrong. They would give her all the time in the world.

The thing Eloise hadn't counted on was that both Rhodes and Tiago had plenty of experience with brats and naughty Little girls. There were always plenty of them staying at the Ranch and several who lived there full-time.

They knew it was best not to overreact. If they lost their tempers or showed any sign of frustration, Eloise would get their reaction stuck in her head and think she'd proven her point.

They couldn't let that happen.

Rhodes took a deep breath and glanced at the clock. It was time to get up and go get his Little girl out of bed. Some days she was still sleeping when he went to get her after her nap. Other days she was awake, lying quietly in her bed with Peaches while she waited on him.

She knew he needed to sleep, and she wasn't permitted to get up until he came to get her. It was hugely telling that even though she usually had a random breakdown every day at some point or another, she respected the two of them enough not to interfere with their sleep.

Rhodes got up, took a quick shower, put on jeans and a T-shirt, and headed for Eloise's nursery.

When he stepped into her room, she turned her head toward him and smiled. "Daddy."

His heart was so full as he came to her. This was one of his favorite parts of the day. She was nearly always sweet and snuggly after her nap. Tiago said the same was true first thing in the morning when he got her up. Their Little girl was at her best when she was rested and freshly awake.

She reached for him as he lowered the side of the bed, and he scooped her into his arms, snuggling her against his body to carry her over to the changing table.

She was so warm and soft. His favorite fifteen seconds

of every day were these right here. Nuzzling her neck, inhaling her scent, feeling her naked breasts against his chest.

Tiago always tucked her in for her nap in nothing but a diaper. She never fussed about the idea and seemed to have relaxed and stopped worrying about them seeing her completely naked while they changed her.

Rhodes's heart beat fast as he removed her diaper and cleaned her folds. It always did. She was so gorgeous. So submissive. So damn perfect. He prayed she was as attracted to the two of them as they were to her.

Evidence would suggest she was, especially when he changed her. Her soft folds were wet and swollen with arousal, her nipples hard little points, and she sometimes arched when he stroked over her clit. Her breath hitched delightfully too.

Neither man had pressured her sexually. They both kissed her and snuggled with her, but they hadn't brought her to orgasm again since that first day.

Rhodes was glad she'd had the experience because it gave her something to think about.

Eloise was particularly wiggly today, and Rhodes had to tighten the strap over her waist to keep her from squirming off the table. While he was adjusting the buckle, she drew her legs together and pulled her knees up. Her hands came to her breasts and covered them at the same time.

Rhodes didn't think any of those actions were conscious decisions. She was panting and aroused, her head tipped back, her mouth open.

Rhodes set his hands on her knees. "Open your legs for me, babygirl," he cooed. "I can't clean you up with your thighs together."

She squeezed her tits with her hands and whimpered as she lowered her gaze to his, blinking. "Will you touch me like you did that one time, Daddy?" Her voice was so soft, he almost couldn't hear her, and she licked her lips afterward, her cheeks flushing. It had been difficult for her to ask for what she wanted.

"I'd be happy to, babygirl." His heart soared. He wanted this with her. This intimacy. It would take time for her to be ready to let one or both of them into her body, but this was a huge step.

He nudged her knees. "Legs, babygirl. Spread them wide so I can see your pretty pussy. I'll make you feel good after I clean you up."

She gasped as she let her knees part.

Damn, she was so fucking precious. His cock was harder than ever watching the way she squeezed her tits in her palms. He kind of wanted to see them, and he considered ordering her hands to her sides or possibly restraining them. But the visual of her pinching her nipples was also fucking hot, so he let her do it.

Besides, it was huge that she'd parted her bent legs for him. He didn't want to push her further.

Holding her pelvis with one hand, he cleaned her folds and tossed the wipe in the trash. Normally, he would unbuckle her, set her on her feet, and dress her now. But she'd asked for more, so he would give her more.

When he parted her lips, she moaned. Her mouth fell open farther when he eased a finger through her wetness and then circled her clit with her arousal.

"Daddy..." Her voice trembled.

"Let it feel good, babygirl. Don't fight it."

Jesus. His heart stopped when Eloise started thumbing her nipples and then pinched them. He truly didn't think she knew she was doing it. Sexiest visual ever.

He pulled the hood away from her clit, held it, and flicked the swollen nub over and over until she stiffened and writhed. As soon as he thought she was near the edge, he thrust one finger up into her.

His cock revolted in his jeans. She was so tight and wet and hot. So exactly perfect. Her pussy clenched down on his finger as if trying to suck it in and keep it.

She cried out the moment he pressed his thumb against her clit, burrowing his finger as deep as possible at the same time.

Rhodes would never in his life forget these moments. Her firsts. All of her firsts. Either he or Tiago would be there to witness every single one, and they would cherish her reactions for the rest of their lives.

He sure as fuck hoped she would still be with them that long too.

Eloise was panting, her body shivering as she came back into herself after the powerful release. She switched from rigid to putty, relaxing onto the changing table.

Suddenly her eyes widened, and she released her pretty tits. "Oh. I…"

Rhodes smiled at her. He bent down to kiss her mound first and then trailed his lips up her body to kiss her pretty nipples.

When he reached her mouth, he kissed her briefly there too. "When both me and Papa are with you, one of us can play with those sweet little nipples while the other one makes your pussy feel good."

She clamped her lips closed and swallowed, embarrassed, just as he'd expected.

He cupped her face. "No reason to be embarrassed, babygirl. I bet your nipples were begging for attention. I only have two hands."

She flushed and glanced away.

Like every single day, he asked her, "Panties or diaper this afternoon?" He always let her choose. She had yet to wear a diaper except for naps and nighttime, but he wanted her to feel like she had options.

He suspected when she got more comfortable, she would spend more time in a younger headspace because she loved being taken care of. But for now, she was only permitting herself to be incredibly young when she was in bed.

It made sense. Rhodes understood. She was alone in bed. She could be who she wanted to without judgment. Letting two men take care of all her needs during waking hours was a giant step. It meant turning over more control. It meant trusting them to handle her with care.

Tiago and Rhodes would always handle her like spun gold. She deserved it. But they needed to let her get there on her own.

"Panties," she whispered as expected.

Without a word, Rhodes unbuckled her, lifted her from the changing table, and settled her on her feet.

She was trembling from the orgasm, and she smelled like sex. It was so heady he was struggling to remain in control of his own needs.

Rhodes helped her into her panties, a yellow cotton dress, and white leggings. After putting white socks on her feet, he grabbed her around the waist and held her against him, kissing all over her face.

She giggled, which pleased him. He wanted her to relax. The orgasm had been intense, and if it was only her second, she was probably feeling out of sorts.

"How about a snack and then I'll read to you, yeah?" He loved reading to her. She listened so intently, eager to find out what happened next in their stories. But more importantly, he loved the way she sat in his lap and snuggled against him while he read.

She nodded. "Can I have cookies?"

He chuckled. "Only if you have something healthy first."

She pouted. "Fine."

"How about some hummus with veggies?" he suggested. They'd learned that she liked hummus.

"Mmm. How about cottage cheese?"

"Excellent choice." Sometimes he felt confident she was testing them to see if they would force her to eat things she wasn't in the mood for. They never fell for that routine. She could choose, as long as it was healthy before sweet.

"Can't I sit on one of the stools like you, Daddy?" she asked as he strapped her into her highchair.

He wondered where this was going. His Little girl always made things interesting. It was hard to keep a straight face because he suspected she was about to give him one of her full meltdowns. She had such a skewed view of what the results of a tantrum would be.

Somehow she thought they would grow tired of her and eventually make her leave. She had no flipping clue that her tantrums were actually adorable most of the time. They were part of her personality. They kept Rhodes and Tiago on their toes. Life was never boring. And Rhodes certainly didn't mind pulling her pants down and spanking her sweet bottom.

"Nope." He tapped her nose as he secured the tray.

"Why not?" she whined.

"Hard rule, babygirl. The stools are high off the ground. I don't want you to fall. That would make me a horrible Daddy."

She rolled her eyes.

Oh, yeah. It was on.

"Daddy... You know I won't fall. I'm not a baby. I won't trip if I run. I won't get hurt playing outside alone. I won't drown in the bathtub either."

He chuckled and gripped the sides of her tray. "Here's what I know, Eloise. I know you enjoy a deep age play and you're testing me. I know you thrive on strict rules and guidance."

She hmphed and crossed her arms. "You don't know anything."

He bent his knees so his face was level with hers. "I know a lot more than you think, babygirl. Daddies know things. For example, I know you're itching to spend more of the day at a younger age but you're afraid to ask for what you want."

She gasped. "You don't know that."

He lifted both brows. "And since you brought it up, tonight Papa and I are going to start giving you baths. After all, we definitely don't want you to drown in the tub."

Her mouth fell open. "You said the bathroom was my private time."

He gave her a slight shrug. "I don't think you need private time anymore. Papa and I have seen your naked body many times. We've touched every inch of you. It's time to extend that to baths."

He watched her reaction closely, knowing he was spot on when her cheeks flushed and she started squirming. "I like showers better," she argued.

It was so hard to keep a straight face. Eloise rarely took a shower. She nearly always ran the bath at night. They could hear her in there playing with the toys they'd left in the tub for her. She made the sea animals talk to each other, and it made Rhodes want to yank open the door and join her.

Starting tonight, new rules. She was more than ready for that change.

Eloise switched topics on him so fast his head spun around. "I don't want cottage cheese. Just cookies."

The way she kept her arms crossed over her chest but lifted her elbows in a dramatic expression before dropping them was so very Eloise.

"Cookies come after the healthy snack. You know that. You choose between hummus, cottage cheese, cheddar wedges, or mozzarella sticks. If not, you can get down, but there won't be cookies." He needed to be firm with her. It was what she craved. It was why she tested them every day.

She shook her head. "You can't make me eat."

"Nope. I sure can't, but I can let you go without a snack altogether."

She gasped. "You would starve me?"

He laughed. It wasn't possible to contain. "I don't think missing one snack will send you to your grave, babygirl. Besides, I'm not the one making the choice not to eat. You are."

Eloise crossed her arms, furrowed her brows, and pushed her bottom lip out in the most adorable pout ever.

What she didn't realize was that she had him wrapped all the way around her finger. He wasn't a pushover. He'd never bend the rules. But that was exactly what she wanted —strict Daddies who didn't bend.

Now what? This afternoon was going to be interesting.

CHAPTER TWELVE

"Do you need another nap, babygirl?" Daddy asked her as Eloise kicked her feet against the legs of the highchair.

She frowned deeper, scowled harder, scrunched her eyes together tighter, and shook her head. "I'm not tired," she insisted. She was wide awake, and her naughty side was about to boil over. She'd been good for too long. She was itching for a confrontation.

Her two Daddies were unflappable. They never got angry. They never gave a single sign they were tired of dealing with her. Her heart was loosening up to them a bit more every day. But she worried. And she pushed.

Eloise had a new game, and she knew it. She liked being held and coddled and kissed. She liked being touched. And sometimes the best touches of all were against her bottom.

She liked getting spanked. So, she misbehaved. No one had spanked her today, and she missed the contact. She wanted Daddy's hand on her bare bottom. She liked how her heart rate increased when he exposed her. She liked how it felt for him to rub her butt cheeks before he started and after he finished.

Papa too. They each had a different style, but she liked both. How lucky was she that she had two Daddies who doted on her all the time?

That thought made her both sad and happy at the same time. She was blessed, but she also knew it could all end in a second. How far could she push them? They both insisted there was no limit, but she didn't believe them.

"I want to get down," she demanded as her naughty pushed harder to the surface.

"Ask nicely then, Eloise," Daddy responded as he went about his business in the kitchen. He took out a mozzarella stick, opened it, and pulled a string off.

Eloise pursed her lips together as he approached her, thinking he would try to get her to eat it, but he popped it in his own mouth instead. She gasped and then dipped her head to her tray again.

"Mmm. This cheese is really good. I should eat string cheese more often. No wonder you like it." He pulled off another string, tipped his head back, and lowered it into his mouth.

She didn't lift her face, but she watched him.

"It tastes better when you pull off the strings than just biting into it. Wonder why?" he commented.

He was right. It did, and she wanted some. No way was she going to let him know though. She wanted cookies more.

Actually, that wasn't true. She didn't care about the cookies. She wanted a spanking. There was always a risk with this behavior. He might put her in timeout instead of spanking her. She hated timeouts. Standing in the corner being ignored was boring.

Being strapped in this highchair wasn't conducive to anything at all. She was going to have to be at least nice enough to get down before she really fell apart. She'd examined the locking mechanism a few times. If she were ever in a bind, she could get out, but reaching around to the front to unfasten the tray wouldn't be easy, and she'd never get away with it while either Daddy was paying attention.

"Please may I get down, Daddy?" she mumbled.

"Of course, babygirl. Thank you for being polite." He popped the last string of cheese in his mouth and then undid her tray before reaching for the buckles at her waist.

The moment he set her on her feet, she stomped from the room.

"Eloise..." he warned. "I don't care if you spend the rest of the day pouting but watch yourself."

She shot him a glare, turned around, and ran to her nursery where she squished herself into the corner next to the bookshelf, drew her knees up, and wrapped her arms around them. She set her chin on her knees and pouted.

Daddy took his time following her, which annoyed her. Eventually, he filled the doorway, hands on his hips. "What's the rule about running in the house, Eloise?"

She ignored him.

He stood there a few more moments before speaking again. "Okay, well, I've got some things to take care of around the house. You can sit there and pout for as long as you want." With that he turned and left.

Eloise felt her naughty side rising closer to the surface with each passing minute. This was nothing. She hadn't decided yet how she wanted to misbehave today. It needed to be epic. Something he couldn't ignore. Something that would make both her Daddies very disappointed.

Something that would end with her bottom bright red, her nose in the corner, and both Daddies rethinking their decision to keep her.

She looked around the room from her tiny corner. She could break something, but she didn't want any of her new toys to be broken. She liked them. She could color on the walls, but the room was too pretty to mark on the paint and ruin it.

She considered sneaking out of the house and wandering away. That would really make them mad. It could also be dangerous. She had no money and nowhere to go. The thought of living on the streets again made her stomach roil.

Hugging her knees tighter, she tried to make herself smaller. Time passed. A lot of it. She wasn't sure how long she huddled in the corner, lonely, in her self-imposed timeout.

She could be with Daddy right now, sitting in his lap, listening to him read. She could be outside playing or in the kitchen having a snack. Instead, she sat here on the floor in her room, her butt hurting from the hard floor.

If she weren't so stubborn, she could at least be wearing a diaper. If her bottom were padded, it wouldn't be so sore. If she had on a diaper, she wouldn't have to worry about needing to crawl out of this corner to use the bathroom either.

Eloise was creating her own problems in her attempt to sabotage the best thing that had ever happened to her. Why couldn't she be brave and take a risk? Let these two amazing Daddies be hers for real?

The lighting in the room began to dim as the sun went down which meant she'd been huddled in her corner for a long time. Suddenly, she heard the sound of the front door opening and closing. She stiffened. No way would Daddy leave the house.

A few minutes later, she peeked toward the door to see too sets of feet entering her room. Not just Daddy but also Papa. Her heart seized. Papa was home. That couldn't be

A CHEERFUL LITTLE COLORING DAY

good. He was supposed to be at work. Maybe this was it, the moment they would tell her she wasn't worth the effort.

Before either of them spoke, tears slid silently down her cheeks and hit her knees. Sadness consumed her. She'd really done it this time. She'd pushed and pushed until they didn't want her.

Both men surprised her when they lowered to the floor in the middle of her room, sitting, facing her, legs crossed.

Papa spoke first. "Daddy told me you were having a rough day, so I came home from work early, sweet girl." His voice was gentle and kind, surprising her.

She flinched and lifted her gaze to his even though she didn't want to. "Why?" She hiccupped, giving away her quiet sobs.

He smiled at her. "Because you're more important to me than anything in the world. We don't want you to be sad, Eloise. It breaks my heart that you're crying. Are you unhappy living with us?"

She gasped and shook her head. How could she be unhappy in their home? It was the best place in the world.

Daddy spoke next. "Your quiet sadness is worse than your tantrums, babygirl. My heart hurts. You've been in here a long time. You're scaring Daddy."

She flinched again. "Why am *I* scaring *you*?"

"Because you've burrowed so deep into my heart that I never want to be without you. It will make me very sad if you decide you don't like living with us and would rather go back to the dorm. If that's what you want, we won't stop you, but we do want you to talk to us first."

Eloise couldn't stop her eyes from going wide. Words rushed out of her mouth before she could stop them. "I don't want to go back to the dorm, Daddy. I want to be here with you and Papa."

He visibly exhaled, the corners of his mouth lifting into a smile.

"But I'm naughty and I don't know why you want to keep me," she continued. "And I got scared because you didn't spank me when I misbehaved."

His eyes widened. "Is that why you're so upset? You thought I'd given up on you when I didn't spank you?"

She nodded, so filled with emotions. Tears ran down her cheeks in a steady stream.

Papa cleared his throat. "All we want, sweet girl, is for you to be happy. We're trying so hard to figure out what makes you happy and give you whatever that is. It's hard because you give us so many mixed signals. It would be easier if you told us exactly what you want."

She swiped at the tears but they kept falling. "I don't want you to send me away."

Daddy shook his head. "We will never ever send you away, Eloise. *Never*. The only way you're going to leave us is if you choose to do so, and even then we will try to talk you out of it. We adore you, and we will fight for you, Eloise."

Papa nodded. "He's right, sweet girl. You've been buried deep in my heart since before you moved in with us. If you left, a piece of me would go with you."

"Why didn't you spank me earlier?" she asked, glancing at Daddy.

"I thought you needed time to think, babygirl. Did you misbehave on purpose because you wanted me to spank you?"

She shrugged and then slowly nodded. "Maybe."

Papa leaned forward, putting his elbows on his knees. "We know you misbehave in order to test our resolve, but maybe there's more to it. Some Little girls really enjoy getting spanked just because."

Eloise frowned. That didn't make any sense.

Daddy nodded. "He's right. Some submissives need a good maintenance spanking every so often. They enjoy the release of endorphins and the intimacy. Do you think maybe you'd feel better if one of us spanked you sometimes without provocation?"

She was still hugging her knees as she glanced back and forth between them. She wasn't entirely sure she understood what he was suggesting.

Papa spoke next. "Daddy has a good point. Some days you really work hard to find a new creative way to end up over our laps. I bet it would be easier if we spanked your pretty bottom once a day without you working so hard to earn it." He lifted a brow.

Eloise stared at him. "Why would you spank me if I wasn't naughty?"

"Because you enjoy being spanked, sweet girl. Instead of working so hard to come up with a way to misbehave, you could just ask one of us to spank you."

She gasped. "That doesn't make sense." Did it? She hadn't seen any other Little girls asking their Daddies to spank them. "Who would do that?"

"Lots of Littles do it," Daddy informed her. "It's more common than you think. Some like a scheduled time when they know their Daddy will swat their bottom. Others like to let their Daddy choose when to take them over his knees. And some Little girls prefer to flat-out ask."

She swallowed. "It hurts my bottom when you spank me," she pointed out. "Why would I ask you to do it?"

Daddy chuckled softly. "It's a good kind of pain though. The kind that helps you relieve your stress. Plus, it makes you squirm every time, babygirl," he pointed out.

Heat rose up her cheeks. She'd hoped he hadn't noticed that fact. It embarrassed her even though both Daddies had told her not to let it. She had trouble wrapping her head around the sensations that welled up inside her when either of them spanked her. It had never been like that with anyone else. Just her Daddies.

"How about if we try it, sweet girl?" Papa suggested. "Every day at least once, one of us will spank you. You don't have to misbehave to earn a spanking. You may still have all the tantrums you like, but they may or may not result in getting your bottom swatted. Daddy and I will decide when to spank you."

Daddy nodded. "I think it's a great idea. And if you find yourself wanting more, all you have to do is ask."

Her mouth fell open. "I don't think I could ever ask you to spank me. That feels weird."

They both chuckled.

"I bet you could," Papa disagreed. He reached out a hand. "Come here, sweet girl. Let's give it a try. I bet you'll feel much better afterward."

She stared at his outstretched hand for a moment before releasing her knees. She winced as she crawled out of her corner, her legs stiff and sore from holding that position for so long.

"That's a good girl," Daddy praised as she inched toward them on her hands and knees, nervous about this plan.

When she got close, Papa reached for the hem of her dress and eased it over her head, leaving her naked from the waist up. It surprised her. They didn't usually take her dress off to spank her.

She shivered as the air hit her breasts, making her nipples pucker. She suddenly wanted them to touch her more than ever before. Their heated gazes roamed over her chest, making her self-conscious. Making her tremble.

Daddy patted the back of her thigh. "Stand up, babygirl."

A CHEERFUL LITTLE COLORING DAY

She rose to her feet, trembling as he drew her closer, reached for the elastic waist of her leggings, and drew both them and her panties down her legs. Moments later, she was naked.

She'd been naked with both of them many times, but they didn't usually linger like this, staring at her so blatantly. In addition, she was standing while Daddy and Papa were sitting. She had to look down at them. Their faces were level with her private parts.

Daddy silently slid his hands up her thighs and over her hips before coming to a stop with his thumbs grazing the underside of her breasts. "You are the prettiest Little girl ever, Eloise." His voice was low and deep.

Papa's hand came to her lower back and slid down to her butt, giving her cheek a squeeze. "He's right. Gorgeous. Even prettier when your bottom is hot pink to match your cheeks." He lifted his other hand to cup her face, making her realize her cheeks were heated.

Suddenly, both men rose to their feet, surprising her. She'd expected them to spank her right there on the floor. Instead, Papa took her hand and led her from the nursery without a word.

She followed right on his heels, Daddy so close behind her that she could feel his body heat. She was surprised when Papa led her into his room. She'd only been in their rooms a handful of times, usually because she was following them around.

Papa's bed was huge. So was Daddy's. But right now they were in Papa's room, and he lifted her off the floor and sat her on the big bed. "Hands and knees, sweet girl," he cooed. "Facing the headboard."

She wasn't used to actively participating in her punishments. But this wasn't a punishment at all. They were going to spank her just because. As soon as she got into the required position, perched near the edge of the mattress, Papa grabbed two pillows and tucked them under her belly, making her shiver.

Daddy slid a hand up her back and pressed between her shoulder blades. "Drop to your elbows, babygirl."

Her arms were shaking, so she was glad for the relief that would provide her, but as soon as she lowered, she realized two things. Her butt was in the air, and her nipples were rubbing against the comforter.

Papa grabbed a third pillow and nudged her knees. "Spread your legs, Eloise."

She parted her thighs farther and nearly moaned when he pushed the pillow between her knees. She was so exposed and vulnerable in this position. Need built in her belly. The tight ball she often experienced clenched harder than ever.

She was wet. So wet her arousal was going to run down her inner thighs. The thought made her feel even more horny. She whimpered as both men stroked her skin, seemingly everywhere except where she most wanted. Her legs, thighs, butt, back, arms.

Daddy cupped the back of her neck and bent down to kiss her temple. "What do you need, Eloise?" he whispered in her ear.

Her lip trembled. He was going to make her ask for it?

"Tell us," Papa encouraged. "Tell us what you want, sweet girl. We will always give it to you."

She swallowed her fear and licked her lips. "I want you to spank me. Both of you. Spank me so hard that it hurts for the rest of the day." Her breath hitched when she was done speaking, shocked by her admission. She'd never fully realized how badly she enjoyed being spanked.

CHAPTER THIRTEEN

Had it always been like this? Even with Master Derek or the others who had spanked her? Was she naughty with everyone all the time just so they would punish her?

She suspected the answer was yes. She misbehaved because she enjoyed the negative attention it gave her. But this was different. She didn't need negative attention. She just needed attention. Craved it deep inside. And release. She needed to come. She wanted them to spank her hard and then...

Would they?

Daddy's hand slid from her neck to her back and then around to cup one of her breasts, weighing the globe in his palm before flicking a finger over her nipple.

Eloise groaned, the sound of her voice shocking her. She gripped the pillow between her knees and pushed her butt higher, begging silently.

Papa smoothed a hand up her inner thigh, causing her breath to hitch. Instead of spanking her, he stroked his fingers through her folds. "So wet," he commented.

Her face heated. Her breathing became labored. "Papa…"

He removed his hand, patted her bottom, and then swatted her several times in a row, too softly. "Like this?" His voice was teasing.

She shook her head against the mattress. If it was possible, she was even more aroused. "Papa…" This time his name came out on a moan.

He lifted his hand and spanked her harder, peppering her cheeks with his palm, never striking in the same spot twice in a row. He spanked her so thoroughly that she was panting by the time he stopped.

She didn't have a chance to catch her breath though, before Daddy picked up where Papa left off. Daddy's palm was slightly larger and he wasted no time adding to the growing burn all over her bottom.

Papa switched places with Daddy, coming around him so he was closer to her head. He ran his fingers through one of her messy pigtails and then reached under her to cup her breast. When he tweaked one of her nipples, she groaned, lifting her head off the bed.

Suddenly, she thought she might come. Neither of them had touched her clit, but she ached with the driving need to orgasm. Her body was trembling. Her nipples were hard, and every time they grazed the comforter, she felt it all the way to her pussy.

Papa switched his attention back and forth between her nipples, pinching and pulling on the hard buds while Daddy continued to spank her.

Her bottom burned so good, and when he started focusing every swat to the spot where her thighs met her butt cheeks, she cried out. She was going to come. Every spank vibrated to her clit.

Without warning, Daddy's hand slid between her legs

and found her soaking pussy. He parted her folds, pressed his thumb against her clit, and thrust two fingers into her tight channel.

She came so hard and so fast her vision blurred. She screamed too, the high-pitched tone of her voice filling the room.

Daddy kept pumping into her, rubbing her clit now, harder and faster as her orgasm morphed into a second one. It took her by surprise, and she arched her back, lifting her head into the air.

As the orgasm subsided, Daddy eased his fingers out of her, gently stroking her swollen folds.

Papa yanked all three pillows out of the way and rolled her onto her back, angling her so her legs hung off the edge of the bed. They didn't stay that way for long though because Papa came between them, lifted them over his shoulders, and lowered his face to her pussy.

Eloise moaned, her hands coming to Papa's shoulders as he licked and sucked her pussy. Her head rolled back and forth. The pressure built again.

Daddy's fingers found her nipple and pinched it hard. "One more, babygirl. Come for Papa. We like to watch your pretty face when you let yourself go."

She whimpered around every moan, the need to come growing irrationally. When Papa shifted his attention to her clit, sucking it, he pushed his fingers into her. The stretch was wider than she'd experienced. He had to be using three fingers this time.

It felt so good. Too good. The room was spinning out of control. So was her heart. When she came, she gripped his shoulders so hard her nails dug into his skin.

The waves of that third orgasm wore her out, leaving her a pile of heavy flesh as it finally receded.

Eloise was panting heavily, blinking to try to focus.

Eventually, she found both her Daddies leaning over her. Smiling. They looked happier than she'd ever seen them, and it pleased her.

A moment later, her face heated. Embarrassment finally reared its head now that she could think. "I want to see you naked," she blurted. It was the only way she could even the playing field. She was often naked with them. She'd never seen either of their erections.

Sometimes one of them had his shirt off, but she'd yet to get a glimpse of anything below the waist. She licked her lips. "I want to touch you too. The way you touch me," she whispered. "Please."

She was relieved when both men pulled their shirts over their heads. *Finally*.

Daddy met her gaze as his hands come to the button on his jeans. "We're not going to make love to you today, Eloise. But you're welcome to explore."

She held her breath, eyes wide as he popped the button and lowered the zipper. She licked her lips as he tugged his jeans and underwear over his hips and down to his thighs.

She gulped as his erection popped free at the same time Papa's did. Shifting her gaze back and forth between them, she held her breath. She'd expected... well, not this. Were penises really that large? She had to assume so since she was now seeing two of them.

It was absurd that she was twenty-four and she'd never seen or touched a man's erection. It was time to put an end to her ignorance.

Rising up, she scooted to the edge of the mattress so she could see them both better. They shed the rest of their clothes and stepped close, flanking her thighs.

Eloise licked her lips as their shafts bobbed in front of her, both men now stroking their erections from base to tip. White liquid pearled on the ends right at their slits.

A CHEERFUL LITTLE COLORING DAY

She wasn't sure who to touch first, and she didn't want either of them to feel slighted, so she lifted both hands to tentatively stroke both mushroom-shaped heads.

The skin was so smooth, and when she glanced up at their faces, she found them both gritting their teeth, looking slightly... pained? She jerked back.

Daddy reached for her hand though, and helped her wrap it around his length. "You aren't hurting us, babygirl."

She glanced at Papa before wrapping her other hand around his erection too, easing her fingers up and down their shafts, learning so much. Smooth, hard skin. Both of their shafts lengthened and grew even harder in her grasp.

Curiosity brought questions to the surface. "I know they aren't always this large. They'd never fit in your pants. How, uh, what do they usually look like?" Her face heated, and she didn't meet their gazes.

Papa let out a strained chuckle. "I doubt you'll ever know, sweet girl."

"Why not?" She finally looked at his face.

He smiled and cupped her cheek, stroking her bottom lip with his thumb. "When you're around, our cocks get hard, Eloise. Unavoidable."

"Oh." She wanted to taste them. Taste the milky cum dripping from the tips. Again, she worried about hurting their feelings, so she slid both the tips of her pointer fingers through their slits, gathered their precum, and brought both fingers to her mouth to suck them at the same time.

Daddy groaned. Well, so did Papa.

She grinned as she lifted her gaze again. "Salty."

They both looked like they might self-combust. It was powerful and invigorating. She did this to them. Feeling bolder still, she cleared her throat. "I know men like to be sucked. Can I do that?"

Renewed wetness gathered between her legs. She really wanted to feel the weight of them between her lips. Papa had just had his mouth on her pussy. It was her turn.

Papa's voice was strained when he spoke. "You can, sweet girl, but if you take me into your mouth, a lot more than a drip of cum is going to come out. I'm so close to orgasm just standing here."

She loved that. It emboldened her further. "I can swallow it then, right?"

He groaned. "If that's something you want to do, yes. It's not a requirement."

Daddy stroked a hand up her arm and then tucked two fingers under her chin to angle her face toward him. "We will never pressure you to do anything you're not comfortable with, babygirl. You're so very innocent and inexperienced. There's no rush. Don't do anything you're not ready for."

She straightened her spine. The fact that they were being so cautious made her feel all warm and gooey inside. She loved them. She knew it. She'd fought against the feeling because it scared her and made her feel vulnerable. But she was losing the battle.

She slid off the bed onto her knees in front of them, bringing her mouth to just the right height. She hadn't had a chance to touch either of them so intimately, so she took the opportunity to slide her hands up their outer thighs and over their tight glutes.

When she applied pressure to their butts, they stepped closer, closing the distance until both erections were in front of her mouth, nearly colliding.

Her men each set a hand on her shoulders.

She flicked her tongue out, managing to lick both cockheads at the same time, marveling at the sounds that came from deep in their throats.

After swirling her tongue around one and then the other in quick succession, she tipped her head back. "Is this okay. Do you..." She swallowed. "Do you care if you're touching each other?" She continued to look up at them as she gripped both erections with her hands and slid up and down the shafts.

Daddy gripped her shoulder. "We aren't interested in each other sexually, babygirl, but in the context of pleasuring you, we don't have any problem bumping into each other."

Good. She didn't want this to be awkward. It was already way out in left field. Two men. Two Daddies. Both of them wanted her. Right? She doublechecked by looking them both in the eyes, shifting her gaze back and forth. All she saw was love and devotion. No pressure. Nothing to indicate they didn't want this.

She could feel their emotions projecting from their expressions and the way they stroked her shoulders.

The salty taste of their cum lingered on her tongue, and she wanted more, so she dipped her head and took. Holding them both in her hands, she suckled one and then the other, switching back and forth.

Nothing in her life had ever felt this powerful. She wanted to take them deeper. She wanted to make them come. She wanted to swallow every drop.

The air seemed to suck out of the room, leaving her panting as she continued to tease them, switching back and forth, licking, tasting, tormenting them. She knew she was affecting them as strongly as she suspected because they kept inching closer, bodies tight and stiff, groans of pleasure coming from both of them.

"Eloise..." Papa's voice held a hint of warning. "Sweet girl, you're going to make us come in a moment. Warning.

That can be in your mouth or against your chest or even to the side."

"I want to swallow you," she murmured before she sucked Papa's incredibly stiff erection as deep as she could. She held him deep, cheeks hollow, for several seconds, knowing he was close.

Instead of finishing him off, she released him and did the same thing to Daddy.

Papa was panting. His hand came over hers around the base of his erection and squeezed. Maybe that helped him keep from coming. Sometimes she could stave off an orgasm by squeezing her muscles tight and holding her breath. Not forever, but for a moment.

When she released Daddy to switch back to Papa, Daddy gripped the end of his cock instead of the base. He didn't say a word, but she felt the strain, the growing need.

Sliding her hand down to the base of Papa's shaft—taking his hand with her over the top—she sucked again, deeper, harder. She eased partly off and did it again.

That was the last straw. Papa's body tensed and he leaned into her, his hand sliding to the back of her head. A second later, hot jets of his cum hit the back of her throat while he groaned deeply in satisfaction.

She swallowed every salty stream of his release and flicked her tongue over the tip for good measure as she eased off.

A second later, her mouth was on Daddy doing the same thing. His hand came on top of Papa's at the back of her head, holding her steady, guiding her as she sucked him just as deeply and hollowed her cheeks again.

Daddy growled as he came against the back of her throat, his fingers tangling in her hair. He arched his hips toward her too, deepening the contact.

When she finally let him slide out of her mouth, she

noticed both erections still bobbed long and hard in front of her. They hadn't deflated at all.

She didn't know who did what, but somehow they managed to lift her off the floor and settle her in the middle of the bed, both men coming to her sides, leaning over her, stroking her everywhere, watching her face.

She flushed as the reality of what she'd done fully sank in. "Did I do it right?" She was teasing.

They both chuckled and took turns kissing her before they each cupped a breast and played with her nipples.

Daddy spoke first. "Nothing has ever been more right in my life."

"Mine either," Papa agreed.

CHAPTER FOURTEEN

Tiago was so proud of Eloise as he held up her sticker chart for all of them to see. It was completely filled in.

It had been several days since their Little girl crawled out of that corner, asked for what she wanted, and got more than she expected. In that time, the three of them had grown gradually close, but neither he nor Rhodes had taken their pants off again.

Yet.

They wanted to give her more time to settle into her life and accept it. Trust them to be there for her always.

They wanted her to be able to look them in the eyes, tell them she loved them, and believe they would never abandon her for any reason. Until then, they'd taken a step back.

Eloise was in her highchair eating pancakes for breakfast. Today was going to be her second day of classes, and she was grinning with excitement as she stuffed another syrup-drenched bite of pancake into her mouth.

Rhodes had put a bib on her, and good thing because already she had sticky syrup dripping down the front of it.

Tiago was beyond pleased. His sweet girl hadn't stopped talking about what she'd learned in class for the rest of the day yesterday. Turned out, once she got over her fear of looking "stupid," she thrived. She loved learning. She was a sponge. She would tackle and conquer her GED in no time.

"Slow down, babygirl," Rhodes said as he pointed at her plate. "And eat the protein on your plate too. Little girls can't learn on just carbs. Eggs and sausage too. And drink your milk."

Tiago leaned against the counter, sipping his coffee, watching his sweet girl as she stabbed into a bite of sausage without complaining or rolling her eyes to test them. Her feet were swinging, pigtails swaying, cheeks glowing.

She was happy.

They were blessed.

Please don't let this boat rock.

"Does this mean we get to go to Coloring Book Day?" she asked as soon as she took a drink of milk.

"Yep. Tomorrow," Tiago informed her. Other than classes at the college, Eloise hadn't spent time at Rawhide Ranch since she'd come to live with them at Rawhide Ridge. She hadn't gone back to work or to the nursery.

"Are you looking forward to seeing your friends? I bet all the Little girls who live at the Ranch and even the guests visiting this week will be at the festivities." Tiago watched her closely, wondering how she felt about mingling with the other Littles again.

She pushed her eggs around for a moment and shrugged. "I guess," she muttered.

Rhodes was sitting closer, and he reached out and tipped her chin up. "Are you nervous about seeing them again?"

She nodded. "I was always mean to them. They don't like me." Her bottom lip trembled.

"I bet that's not true. I know for a fact that Master Lawson's Little girl, Brooke, wants to be friends," Rhodes said.

"And I'm willing to bet both Sadie and Hayleigh are just waiting for you to make a move letting them know you're open to being friends as well," her Papa added.

"Exactly," Rhodes agreed. "Besides, I haven't met a single Little at Rawhide Ranch who ever held a grudge. If you're worried about how they might have perceived you in the past, why don't you simply apologize. I'd bet my last dollar they will welcome you into their group with a clean slate."

She sniffled. "I don't know," she murmured.

Rhodes took the fork from her hand and lifted a bite of eggs to her lips.

Luckily, she accepted the bite and swallowed her food.

Tiago wet a washcloth and came toward them, prepared to clean her sticky fingers when she was finished. He pulled a stool over to her side. All he wanted was for her to be happy, and she probably needed a pep talk.

When she finished letting Rhodes feed her the last bite and drained her milk, Rhodes took her dishes while Tiago wiped her face and then hands. He met her gaze, not wanting to release her until they talked. "I have a suggestion."

She stared at him, eyes wide. "What, Papa?"

"I know you like to test your boundaries. It's in your nature, and neither Daddy nor I want you to stop doing so. It releases your stress when you misbehave and accept your punishments. It's part of who you are. We know that, and we like that side of you."

She nodded. He thought she was starting to understand more about herself.

He continued, "You have a new tool now though. You

also know you can come to either of us at any time and ask for a spanking if you need the release. You don't always have to invent a naughty behavior to get what you need.'

She nodded again, listening intently. They'd come a long way.

"How about if you try another new tactic to get your needs met? How about if when you're with other Littles, you save up your urges to misbehave and redirect them. Instead of knocking over another Little girl's block tower, for example, you could choose another option," he suggested.

"Like what?" she asked, listening intently still.

"You have three choices. If Daddy or I are nearby, you could come to us and ask us to discipline you. If we're not around, you could hold on tight to the urge to misbehave until we're back at the house later. Or, if you really can't wait, you could have a tantrum that isn't directed at anyone else."

Tiago liked the way she was watching him, absorbing his suggestions, mulling them over in her mind. "You mean like refusing to go down for a nap or pouting in the corner when it's time to line up?"

Tiago smiled. "Exactly. Those are both good choices that don't hurt anyone else's feelings. If you're in the Caterpillar Room, Nanny J or another attendant can call one of us to come discipline you, send you to Master Derek's office, or spank you themselves. Your behavior wouldn't be directed at another Little."

She gave him a huge grin. "I think I can do that."

He leaned over, kissed her on the lips, and then touched his forehead to hers. "I know you can. Now, shall we get you to school? I know you don't want to be late."

"Yes, Papa. And tomorrow I'll tell the other Littles I'm

A CHEERFUL LITTLE COLORING DAY

sorry for being mean to them and maybe they will color with me and play games with me, and I won't be lonely."

Tiago tapped her nose. "You'll never ever be lonely again because Daddy and I will always be nearby. No matter what happens, you'll know inside that you only have to wait a short while for one of us to come get you. You'll always have twice the love of anyone around you. Double the hugs and cuddles. Double the fun." He grinned hugely, hoping she could feel his love.

She returned the bright smile, glancing back and forth between him and Rhodes. "You're not going to leave me," she whispered as if saying it out loud might help her believe it.

"Never," Rhodes confirmed as he reached over to remove her tray and unfasten her buckle.

Tiago lifted her into his arms, loving how she wrapped her legs around his waist and held on to his neck. She didn't say anything as she set her head on his shoulder and squeezed as tight as she could.

Tiago choked up as he rubbed her back. She was his. She was their Little girl. She was starting to trust and believe it would be forever.

He knew tomorrow would be challenging for her, but he truly believed the other Little girls would welcome her with open arms. All she had to do was apologize for her past behavior and everything would be smooth sailing.

CHAPTER FIFTEEN

Eloise held on very tight to her Daddies' hands as they entered the grassy area where the event was being held. It was late in the summer, and since there were no other fun holidays at this time of year, Littles all over Rawhide Ranch were excited to enjoy this fun day of exciting activities.

Eloise might not have realized what a big deal it was going to be had she not started attending classes where the other Littles had been talking about it nonstop.

She was excited, but also nervous. She'd had trouble falling asleep last night as she'd pondered her Daddies' suggestion to apologize to the other Littles and make amends.

She could do it. She wasn't an inherently mean Little girl. She liked all the Littles she'd met at Rawhide Ranch. The reason for her constant misbehavior had been born out of fear of rejection and a deep desire to receive negative attention over no attention at all. She understood that much better now.

But what if the other Littles rejected her?

Papa and Daddy felt confident no one would turn away from her apology, but uncertainty still made her nervous.

Daddy had worked last night and slept only a few hours this morning so both he and Papa could take her to the festivities. Papa would need to leave them in a few hours to start working himself. She had this special time nestled in the middle of the day with both of them.

Daddy squeezed her hand before bending down to lift her up into his arms, propping her on one hip as they made their way toward the huge bounce house she could see. "Papa said you had trouble falling asleep last night and he had to come in and rub your back several times. Was your tummy upset, babygirl?"

She shook her head. "I was worried about today. What if the other Little girls don't like me?" she asked, fretting for the millionth time.

Her Papa had been amazing last night. He'd babied her exactly how she liked at nighttime, starting with a bath, then a diaper, and snuggly pajamas. He'd rocked her for a long time, feeding her a warm bottle and reading to her, helping her slide into her Littlest head space, the place she most longed to be, especially at night.

Even with all that, she'd tossed around for a while, unable to keep her mind from wandering to visions of rejection.

Suddenly, as they were just about to enter the carnival-like outdoor party, three Little girls she knew well rushed over toward her. They looked excited, grinning wide and clapping their hands.

Sadie jumped up and down. "Eloise! You're here! I'm so glad. I haven't seen you in forever. We've missed you in the cafeteria and the Littles' wing."

Eloise was shocked speechless as Daddy slid her down his body so she stood on her feet. He kept her close, flat-

A CHEERFUL LITTLE COLORING DAY

tening her back to his front, one hand over her shoulder, his palm planted on her tummy.

Her heart was racing and she started wringing her fingers together as Hayleigh and Brooke excitedly agreed.

Eloise had her jaw hanging open as Brooke spoke next. "We were worried about you. I heard you started taking classes at the college though. That's so fun."

"My Daddy and I have missed you in the kitchen," Hayleigh added.

"She means *she* misses sneaking tastes of those fabulous desserts you made," Sadie teased, bumping hips with Hayleigh.

"The playground isn't the same without you," Brooke stated. She started giggling as she leaned in conspiratorially. "No one has made a fuss in the sandbox to keep it exciting in days," she declared.

Eloise's eyes went wide as she remembered how Master Derek had tied the two of them together in order to teach a lesson about how working as a team to build a huge sandcastle was better than fighting. "Oh." She didn't know what to say, but Daddy patted her tummy, his hand reminding her what she'd rehearsed several times. "I uh. I wanted to apologize actually."

All three girls narrowed their eyes in confusion. "For what?" Brooke asked.

Eloise drew in a deep breath and let it all out. "For being naughty all the time and mean. I know I was never a good friend to anyone. I hurt people's feelings when I wouldn't share toys or disrupted everyone's fun with my tantrums. I'm really sorry. I hope you and the others can forgive me and give me another chance." She bit into her lower lip as she watched their expressions change from confusing to shock to smiles.

Daddy released Eloise as Brooke leaned forward to give

her a big hug. "Nothing to apologize for, Eloise. I've always loved your antics. They keep things interesting. That's just who you are." She shrugged as she leaned back. "Some Littles like to misbehave. Nothing wrong with that. You're certainly not alone. I misbehave all the time in lots of ways."

Hayleigh winced as she grabbed Eloise's hand and gave it a squeeze. "Me too. I was so naughty this morning that my Daddy almost didn't let me come to Coloring Book Day. My bottom is too sore to sit down still."

Sadie grabbed Eloise's other hand. "They're right. No need to worry. We all love you. Maybe you could come to the bounce house with us? Several other Littles are in there jumping and laughing and having fun. After that we were going to go to the coloring contest, if you want to join us."

Eloise felt lighter than she had in days as she twisted her head around to look up into her Daddies' faces. They beamed down at her. "Can I Daddy? Papa? Can I go with them to the bounce house?"

"Of course, babygirl," Daddy said as he leaned down to kiss her.

Papa pulled her into his arms, bent to nuzzle her neck, and whispered in her ear, "I told you it would all be fine. I'm so glad to see you smiling. Go play with your friends. We'll watch."

Eloise bounced up and down as Brooke took her hand and led her toward the bounce house. She glanced over her shoulder to see both her Daddies beaming at her with pride.

"Stay where we can see you, babygirl. After the bounce house, make sure you check in with us before you move to another station," Papa stated firmly.

Eloise had never felt so loved in her life. The stern looks on both men's faces were more than she could ever

A CHEERFUL LITTLE COLORING DAY

have imagined for herself. They loved her. They hadn't said it yet, but she knew they loved her. She could see it in their faces.

As she glanced between them, skipping toward the bounce house, she felt happier than ever, and she prayed this was what her life would be like from now on. Two men who adored her and made rules for her. Babied her and cared for her. Disciplined her and gave her so much pleasure.

She was still grinning as she climbed into the bounce house. That's when the smile changed to laughter as all the Littles jumped as high as they could, pigtails flying, dresses flouncing up and down, socked feet slipping out from under them.

When they were exhausted from bouncing, they slid out and put their shoes back on. They were heading for the coloring contest next.

Eloise lifted her gaze and looked around for her Daddies. For a moment, she panicked when she couldn't readily see them nearby. What if they'd gotten bored waiting for her? What if they'd found something better to do?

Her chest tightened as she spun around, scared, panic rising.

And then she saw them coming toward her and blew out a long breath of relief. She'd grown to expect them to be nearby.

Daddy reached her first and swept her off her feet. He held her against his chest and kissed all over her face before leaning back and smiling. "It's so good to see you so happy." His expression froze and changed to one of concern. "What's the matter, babygirl?"

Papa's hand landed on her back. His brow was furrowed.

"I was scared when I couldn't see you." She wrapped her arms around both of them so tight, pulling them in close. "I thought maybe you'd found something better to do than wait for me to finish in the bounce house."

"Never," Papa reassured her.

Daddy adjusted her so that both men were holding her up in their arms. He kissed her gently on the lips. "I love you, Eloise. I will never walk away from you."

"I love you too, sweet girl. Forever," Papa added. "You'll never need to panic again. One or both of us will always be close by. You'll never be alone."

Tears ran down her cheeks as she met both their gazes back and forth. "I love you too, Papa and Daddy."

They both kissed her face again and then let her slide down to her feet.

"No crying today," Papa stated. "It's a fun day. Let's head for the coloring contest. I want you to draw us the prettiest picture ever."

Eloise bit her bottom lip and looked up at them. "I'm not that great at coloring. You won't be disappointed if I don't win, will you?"

They both chuckled. Daddy tugged one of her pigtails. "No matter what, to us, your picture will be the best in the world. You've already won as far as we're concerned."

She smiled broadly as Hayleigh shouted behind her, "Eloise, come on! We're going to miss it!"

Turning around, she found her friends waiting for her, all of their Daddies also hovering nearby. She let Brooke and Hayleigh grab her hands and ran with them and Sadie into the coloring tent to find a spot.

Every once in a while, she glanced up to look for her Daddies but they were always right where she'd left them, sitting in a cluster with several other Daddies. At least one of them was always watching her as if they took turns, making sure she was never out of sight.

So much love flowed between them that she didn't even care if her picture was any good. All she cared about was that from now on National Coloring Book Day would be her favorite day of the year.

A day her world changed when she apologized to her friends and found acceptance in their lives. A day her Daddies both told her they loved her. A day filled with too many snacks and lots of laughs.

A day she hoped would end in their bed, curled in their arms after they made love to her. That was the only thing missing from her life, and she felt confident they would give her that part of themselves after all the fun was over and they got back home.

CHAPTER SIXTEEN

※

That wasn't how it happened, however. For one thing, Papa had to leave them in the middle of the afternoon to go work his shift. For another thing, Eloise was exhausted when she and Daddy got back to the house. She'd barely been able to keep her eyes open as Daddy went through the motions of feeding her, giving her a bath, reading to her, and encouraging her to take a bottle.

When he tucked her into bed with Peaches in her arms, she could barely hold her eyes open. "Thank you for the best day ever, Daddy," she murmured.

"You're welcome, babygirl." He kissed her cheek, lingering for so long that she was asleep before he left her room.

When Eloise woke up the next morning, Papa was there to take care of her. Daddy was asleep. He hadn't gotten more than a few hours of rest the previous day, so they needed to tiptoe around the house and not disturb him.

Papa kept his voice to a whisper as he laid her on the changing table and pulled the strap over her. "No school today, sweet girl," he pointed out as he wiped her folds gently. He met her gaze and asked the same question they both asked every time she woke up in the morning or from a nap. "Diaper or panties?"

She drew in a slow breath. "Diaper, Papa."

As if this weren't a shocking change of events, Papa simply put a clean diaper on her. When he was finished, he lifted her up, set her on the floor, and pulled a pink cotton dress over her head. "There. Let's see about breakfast."

She pursed her lips as he led her from the nursery, trying to control her heart rate. This was a big decision. The diaper made her waddle. It made her feel younger too and pushed her into a deeper age-play mindset.

Papa settled her in her highchair before fixing breakfast. Instead of putting her plate on the tray and giving her a fork, he sat next to her and fed her himself as if this were their everyday routine.

Since it wasn't a school day, Papa let her play all morning, mostly out back where he joined her in the sandbox for a while and then spread out her art supplies on the table in the shade.

She hadn't won the coloring contest yesterday, but her Daddies had hung her picture on the fridge, oohing and ahhing over it as if it were the best one they'd ever seen.

When Papa brought a cup of sand from the sandbox to the table and set it next to her, she looked up at him and furrowed her brow. "What's that for?"

He smiled. "Seems like you're on a beach theme this week. I thought you could glue some real sand onto your pictures."

She grinned. "That's a great idea."

He slid into the chair next to her and tucked a stray lock of hair behind her ear. "Maybe you'd like to do a beach theme in your bathroom too. What do you think?"

She turned her gaze to him again. "I would love that,

A CHEERFUL LITTLE COLORING DAY

Papa," she said softly. It felt like he'd read her mind. A few weeks ago, she wouldn't have dared actually changing anything in the house because she'd been afraid she would lose it all eventually. But that fear had ebbed and only snuck up on her for short periods of time lately.

"I spoke to Chef Connor yesterday," Papa said, changing the subject. "He asked me if you were thinking about coming back or if he should hire someone else to fill your shoes in the kitchen."

Eloise leaned back in her chair and stared at her lap.

Papa kept talking. "I told him we would check with you but that you'd started taking classes and probably didn't have enough time to work." Papa cupped her face and tipped her head back. "I don't want you to feel pressured. Not by us or anyone else. If working is something you enjoy, we'll rearrange your schedule so you can do both."

She licked her lips. "I feel guilty when I'm not working," she admitted. "You are both spending money on me, and I'm not contributing."

He slid closer and kissed her gently. "We don't want you to worry about money. Put it out of your mind. We'd rather you focus on your classes. You're such a good student, bright and eager. I know it's only been a few days, but you're enjoying learning. That's far more important in the long run."

"It doesn't feel like work to me when I'm focused on creating edible art," she pointed out. "I kind of miss that part."

He smiled. "You're certainly good at it. Maybe you could do some of your creations here at the house. We could take them to your friends some days. How does that sound?"

Her face felt like it was going to split open from smiling. "Really?"

"Yep. I think it's a great idea."

"But I'm not even permitted to touch things in the kitchen," she pointed out, wondering how this could work.

Papa chuckled. "That's part of your age-play dynamic. We could set aside part of your day to step out of that deep submission so you can be your creative adult side."

She beamed. "Really?"

"Of course. You can make a list of what you need on the fridge and one of us will pick up your supplies from the store each week."

She jumped down from her chair and threw herself at Papa, wrapping her arms around his neck and hugging him tightly. "Thank you, Papa."

He parted his legs and pulled her between them, running his hands up and down her back. His gaze was serious and intense when she finally leaned back to look at him. "I meant what I said yesterday, Eloise. I love you to pieces."

"I love you too, Papa."

His hands slid up into her hair and he brought her lips to his, kissing her deeply, angling his head to one side so he fit together with her so perfectly.

She was panting when they finally broke apart. She held his gaze, needing to admit something. "I love being your babygirl, but I don't think I like to mix my baby side with sex. It feels weird to kiss you like that while I'm wearing a diaper."

He continued to hold her gaze as he lifted her dress with both hands, unfastened the sides of her diaper, and whisked it away, leaving her completely bare under her dress. "Better?" He gave her a sexy grin as he slid his hands up under the hem of her skirt to cup her bottom.

"Much." Her heart was racing. She liked this playful, sexy side of her Papa. She liked the way his hands were trailing up her back now and then slid around to cup her breasts. She gasped when he pinched her nipples.

He slid the dress over her head a second later. "That's even better," he declared. "And I think we need to wake your Daddy up before we take this any further." He stood and swooped her up into his arms before she could respond.

Eloise squirmed in his embrace. "Won't Daddy be mad? He needs his sleep."

"He knew this might happen this morning. He'll be disappointed if we leave him out."

Eloise gasped. "You knew we might end up kissing?"

Papa chuckled as he carried her into the kitchen and continued through the house. "You're kind of irresistible, and now that you keep telling me you love me, I want to make you fully mine in every way. Daddy does too. Are you ready for that, sweet girl?" He paused outside Daddy's bedroom door, meeting her gaze.

"Yes. So much."

Papa knocked on the door, but he opened it a moment later without waiting for a response. Eloise bet the two of them had planned this seemingly impromptu event and that Papa had waited as long as he could this morning to make his move so that Daddy could sleep as many hours as possible.

The room was dark, the only light streaming in from the door they'd just entered. It was enough for Eloise to make out the figure of her Daddy where he lay on his stomach. His hands were up under his pillow. His head was facing toward her. The sheets were down around his waist.

Eloise licked her lips as Papa approached. Daddy didn't have a shirt on, and his back was so smooth and sexy.

He blinked awake as they reached his side. A smile spread across his face as he scooted back, rolled to his side, and pulled the covers out of the way. He patted the mattress next to him. "Someone's naked."

She glanced down at his waist where the sheet no longer covered him. "I don't think I'm the only one."

Papa lowered her to the bed, and Daddy immediately pulled her close to his side and cupped her face. "I think your Papa needs to join us, don't you?"

She glanced back to find Papa already pulling his shirt over his head with one hand while the other popped the button on his jeans.

Daddy scooted across the bed even farther, dragging her with him to make room for Papa. He slid his hand up into her hair and captured her lips in a steaming hot kiss that made every inch of her body tingle and throb before he was done.

Actually, she continued to tingle because Papa's hand was on her thigh, sliding up and down, brushing against her labia and making her squirm.

Daddy's hand was on her too, cupping a breast before he leaned over to suckle the stiff nipple.

Eloise moaned as her body came fully alive with the need that had been growing and building for days.

Daddy trailed kisses to her ear. "Are you sure about this, babygirl? We won't ever let you go after we've made love to you."

"Promise?" she asked, her voice barely a whisper.

"You're ours, Eloise Grace," Papa growled in his sexy voice before he latched on to one of her nipples to resume sucking where Daddy left off.

Daddy jerked the sheet out of the way so he could crawl down the bed and climb between her legs. He parted her thighs wide, wrapped his arms under them, held her down, and dragged his tongue through her folds.

Eloise would have bolted off the bed if he hadn't been holding her so firmly.

Papa cupped her other breast as his mouth nibbled a path to hers, taking her lips in a heated kiss.

It was hard to focus on returning the kiss with Daddy flicking his tongue over her clit. She was climbing the cliff so fast the room started to spin. And then she was right there, tipping over the edge, crying out as her orgasm consumed her.

Papa released her lips as she nearly screamed her release. "You're so gorgeous, Eloise," he murmured reverently. "I need to be inside you."

"Please," she whimpered as Daddy continued to tongue her, keeping her on the edge as one orgasm threatened to turn into two.

Papa leaned away from her for a moment. She heard the drawer of the nightstand opening, and then he was back, several condoms in his hand.

She couldn't keep from grinning as he dropped all but one on the mattress beside her. He lifted the last one up to his mouth and tore the foil package open as Daddy climbed up her body.

Daddy pushed the condoms out of the way and dropped down on his side next to her. He cupped her face and claimed her lips.

Her taste was all over his mouth. It was heady. She wanted more. She wanted everything. It would seem they were going to give it to her.

Daddy lifted his face to stare down at her. His hand was on her tummy, but he slid it down between her legs as Papa rolled the condom onto his erection. "Look at me," Daddy ordered.

She jerked her gaze to his as he thrust two fingers into her tight pussy.

She gasped, her mouth falling open. They'd fingered her before, but not enough. The stretch was tight. Papa's cock was going to be tighter.

Daddy held her pelvis in place with his palm while he thrust his fingers as deep as he could over and over, adding a third without warning. "Spread your legs wider, Eloise."

She obeyed, parting her thighs as far as possible as Papa climbed between them.

Papa was on his knees, his enormous erection bobbing between them as he slid his hand down to join Daddy's. He added a finger, pushing it deep while Daddy kept stretching her.

Eloise couldn't breathe. It felt so good. The stretch was perfect. Tight but not painful.

As if they'd choreographed this scene, both hands disappeared at the same time. Papa dropped between her legs, lined himself up with her channel, and met her gaze. "I love you, Eloise."

"I love you too, Papa." Maybe it would be appropriate to call him by his real name, Tiago, right now, but it didn't feel right. That's not what she ever called him. Master and then Papa. He was her Papa. And she wanted him.

She lifted her hips off the bed.

Papa drew in a breath, cupped her face with both hands, held her gaze, and thrust into her.

She cried out at the shock of the intrusion. There was a moment of discomfort, but it passed so fast she forgot about it. All that was left was the fullness, the ringing of her ears as her heart beat faster, and the intensity of Papa's gaze.

She glanced at Daddy. His face was right there, not missing anything. His hand slid up between them to cup her breast and fondle her nipple.

Eloise gasped as Papa pulled almost out and thrust back

in again. There were no words to describe how full she felt. Complete. Almost complete.

And then Papa was gone.

She whimpered as he dropped to her side, confused until Daddy took his place between her legs. He was at her entrance and inside her so fast there was almost no time between being filled with Papa and then Daddy.

She grabbed his ass, her short nails digging into his firm butt cheek. Her focus was on his face as he dropped his forehead to hers and eased in and out of her.

"Eloise..." Her name on his lips was filled with reverence. "Baby..." He groaned, the sound coming from deep in his chest as he held himself steady, his cock buried to the hilt, his body jerking.

She realized he was coming, and he was still pulsing as he jerked out of her and traded places with Papa.

So much testosterone in this room.

Her channel was full again. Three more thrusts from Papa. Then four. Then his orgasm consumed him too as he let out a guttural sound not unlike Daddy's.

Both men were panting as Daddy's hand snaked between her and Papa to find her clit. He circled it before rubbing it rapidly while Papa was still inside her.

"Come around my cock, sweet girl," Papa demanded as he dropped his lips to take one of her nipples into his mouth, suckling and then grazing it with his teeth.

Eloise's eyes rolled back as Daddy's lips landed on her ear. "Come, babygirl." He pinched her clit at that moment, and she came apart at the seams.

Her body writhed as the waves of her orgasm milked Papa's erection. His own orgasm hadn't caused his shaft to shrink at all, filling her so full that she could feel her channel grasping at him. Holding on to him.

Heaven.

As she floated back to Earth and Papa eased out of her, she knew she had a silly grin on her face. She didn't care. She was so happy.

Both men doted on her, kissing her all over, making her giggle eventually as they licked, teased her nipples, nipped at her skin.

"Do you believe us now?" Daddy whispered in her ear.

"You're ours, Eloise," Papa added. "Forever and always."

"Forever and always," she responded as she drifted into a peaceful sleep nestled between her two Daddies.

CHAPTER SEVENTEEN

Two weeks later...

"I have a message from Master Derek, saying he wants to meet with me," Eloise declared as she sat in her highchair waiting for breakfast. "I wonder what he wants. I don't think I've done anything at school to get into so much trouble that I deserve a spanking from Master Derek."

She was concerned though. She worried her lower lip as she tried to think about why he might want to see her.

Daddy tipped her chin back as he fastened a bib around her neck. He chuckled. "You've been with us a month, babygirl. He told you that was how long he wanted you to give us a chance. Today's your opportunity to back out if you're tired of us."

Papa scowled as he set a plate of food on the island. "You better not be tired of us, or I'll spank some sense into you."

Eloise giggled. "I'll never be tired of you, but you can

still spank some sense into me if you'd like."

Daddy laughed. "That can be arranged." He bent to kiss her lips before heading for the fridge.

Mornings were her favorite. She got both Daddies most mornings at least for a while. Though she was developing individual relationships with both of them that grew with each passing day, she still relished the times when all three of them were together.

On the other side of the island, Papa reached into his computer bag and pulled out a flyer which he dropped on the counter before turning to pour a cup of coffee.

Eloise strained to see what it was, pushing on the sides of her tray to lift herself the scant inch she could manage since she was strapped onto the highchair.

She thought she saw a beach on the flyer and got excited. "Is that for the bathroom, Papa?"

Daddy chuckled. "Nope. Everything for your beach bathroom has already been ordered." He reached for the flyer and slowly slid it across the island until he finally picked it up and handed it to Eloise.

She held it in her hands, scanning the entire thing. Her mind took in the beach first and then a roller coaster, followed by animals. An amusement park? A zoo? The top of the flyer said Littleworld.

She glanced up to find both Daddies grinning at her. "What is this?"

"It's a vacation spot for Littles who enjoy fully regressed age play."

She jerked her gaze back to the flyer, her hands shaking. "It's an island?"

"Yes," Daddy said. "We thought we could take you there for vacation after you finish your GED to celebrate how hard you've been working."

She gasped, her eyes going wide as she looked back and

forth between both men.

Papa chuckled. "I think we've shocked her speechless."

She blinked several times and then started bouncing in her seat. "Are you serious?" Her voice squeaked.

"Very serious."

She opened the flyer to read more about this place. "There's a zoo and an amusement park and a water park and a beach!"

"There sure is. Does it look too boring?" Papa asked, teasing.

Eloise started to cry. She couldn't help it. Her bottom lip trembled. "You mean it?" Her voice shook. "You'd really take me there?"

Both Daddies came to her, stroking her arms and cheeks.

Daddy kissed her. "Of course, babygirl. We're really going to take you there."

"I've always wanted to go to the beach," she whispered, still struggling to believe this was real. That any of this was real.

"You can walk in the sand in the day and in the evening and find out how it really feels on your tootsies when it's not in a sandbox," Daddy pointed out as he wiped her tears away.

Eloise dropped the flyer and wrapped her arms around both men, holding them as close as she could with the highchair tray in the way. "Thank you," she whispered, too choked up to utter more. "I'm the luckiest Little girl in the world."

She meant every word. She truly was. The very luckiest Little girl alive. She had found not one but two Daddies who adored her and would never leave her. She knew it deep in her soul. They would never abandon her. She was finally home.

AUTHOR'S NOTE

I hope you enjoyed A Cheerful Little Coloring Day! It's so fun writing in the Rawhide Ranch world! If you'd like to try one of my other series, I have several, and the list keeps growing. Watch for more books coming soon!

Littleworld
Anabel's Daddy
Melody's Daddy
Haley's Daddy
Willow's Daddy
Juliana's Daddy
Tiffany's Daddy
Felicity's Daddy
Emma's Daddy
Lizzy's Daddy
Claire's Daddy
Kylie's Daddy
Ruby's Daddy
Briana's Daddies
Jake's Mommy and Daddy

AUTHOR'S NOTE

Luna's Daddy
Littleworld Box Set One
Littleworld Box Set Two
Littleworld Box Set Three
Littleworld Box Set Four

Holidays at Rawhide Ranch
Felicity's Little Father's Day
A Cheerful Little Coloring Day

Would you like to see a map of the island?! This link will take you there!

Map of Regression Island and Littleworld

Other books by Paige Michaels:

The Nurturing Center
Susie
Emmy
Jenny
Lily

Eleadian Mates
His Little Emerald
His Little Diamond
His Little Garnet
His Little Amethyst
His Little Sapphire
His Little Topaz

Little Cakes
(by Pepper North and Paige Michaels)
Rainbow Sprinkles

AUTHOR'S NOTE

Lemon Chiffon
Blue Raspberry
Red Velvet
Pink Lemonade
Black Forest
Witch's Brew
Pumpkin Spice
Santa's Kiss

ABOUT THE AUTHOR

Paige Michaels is a USA Today bestselling author of naughty romance books that are meant to make you squirm. She loves a happily ever after and spends the bulk of every day either reading erotic romance or writing it.

Follow Paige on Facebook

Join her newsletter to keep up with her latest releases: Paige's Newsletter Sign-up

Visit her website at PaigeMichaels.com

Follow Paige Michaels on BookBub

Follow Paige Michaels on Goodreads

- facebook.com/PaigeMichaelsAuthor
- amazon.com/author/PaigeMichaels
- bookbub.com/authors/paige-michaels

Made in the USA
Columbia, SC
13 February 2025